Tomb(e)

HÉLÈNE CIXOUS

TRANSLATED BY LAURENT MILESI

LONDON   NEW YORK   CALCUTTA

This work is published with the support of
Institut français en Inde – Embassy of France in India

Seagull Books, 2020

Originally published as *Tombe* by Hélène Cixous, 1973
© Éditions du Seuil, 1973, 2008

First published in English translation by Seagull Books, 2014
English translation © Laurent Milesi, 2014

ISBN 978 0 8574 2 754 0

British Library Cataloguing-in-Publication Data
A catalogue record for this book is available from the British Library

Typeset Seagull Books, Calcutta, India
Printed and bound by WordsWorth India, New Delhi, India

Tomb(e)

THE
SEAGULL
LIBRARY OF
FRENCH
LITERATURE

CONTENTS

One of the greatest challenges in translating *Tombe* is that Cixous' narrative is an infinite orchestration of ever-recombining motifs, often working away at the most resistant idiomatic core of the French language, across polysemy, homonymy and homophony. The reader of the original—and, with him/her, the translator—is thus forced into the kind of hyperamnesia Jacques Derrida had identified as the ineluctable condition of the reader of James Joyce's works (especially *Finnegans Wake*): to become the memory of the text as it retells itself—here as the book which is being written instead of *Tombe* (pp. 24, 109).

However, such a condition is well-nigh impossible in the case of a foreign reader, let alone when such an 'untranslatable' work, trading in idiomaticity, is at stake since the polysemic and polyphonic networks woven in the original can only unravel in another language, no matter how faithful the translator manages to remain.

The chance and event of the republication of *Tombe* at the Seuil in 2008 afforded Hélène Cixous the possibility of retrospective memories, which now do duty as a preface to the fiction itself and which, being by implication of a more (self-)critical nature, have allowed the translator to avail himself of the tacit protocol, which applies to non-fiction writing, for alerting the reader to what inevitably gets 'lost in translation'—signalling original cruxes between square brackets as well as adding a few explanatory notes.

No such protocol is usually resorted to for fiction (unless in the case of critical editions), since it is assumed that such external intervention would distract the reader's immersion in the imaginary processes of story-telling. Yet it was felt that some compromise had to be reached if the translation were to convey in some measure the experience of reading the original text. For the sake of discreet convenience, a glossary of homophones has therefore been provided at the end of the volume and reference to it will be indicated by an asterisk for the first occurrence in the text.

PROLOGUE

Memories of Tomb(e)★

'Tombe lay asleep at the Seuil publishing house,'[1] I wrote this in the night of 15 August 2007. It could have been a dream, a sentence in a text. Tombe, somebody male or female who would be called Tombe. All of a sudden Tombe wakes up, has woken up, like a volcano.[2]

★ The title puns on Châteaubriand's famous memoirs (*Mémoires d'Outre-Tombe*), recalled soon after; but, as the preface reveals, the emphasis shifts to memories which may inhabit a grave (*tombe*) or tomb, hence the translation. Whenever necessary, including for the main title of the *récit* (narrative), the form 'Tomb(e)', with 'e' bracketed off, has been chosen as a makeshift compromise indicating that this tomb or grave also needs to be heard as the French imperative for 'to fall' (French *tombe*), maybe even a fall into such a grave (see below). [Trans.]

1 *Seuil* also means 'threshold' in French. [Trans.]

2 Here and elsewhere Cixous plays on grammatical genders in French which cannot be rendered into English. Hence the 'male or female' addition in order to make up for those bisexual formulations which had to be left out of the translation. [Trans.]

1

Tombe is a book and a grave [*tombe*]. Both. A grave can be a book. A book is a kind of grave which bears within itself the secrets of resurrection. Reading is the priest officiating over this magic. This is not a tomb [*tombeau*]. Not a literary Tomb. *Tombe* is at the Seuil. René de Ceccatty offers to republish this book which appeared in 1973. *Tombe* is exhausted, out of print [*épuisé ou épuisée*]? Tombe is a feminine word? Yes. No. Tombe is a verb. Tombe is absolutely not a silent grave, contrary to popular belief. No more than Sleep, this Somnis which merely sleeps in Book XI of the *Metamorphoses*, so close to a re-emergence of the Lethe in its cave of silence and quiet. Tombe is stirring.

Tombe, the word, says more than a word. *Tombe* as the book's title is totally undecidable. What does one do when one calls a book *Tombe*? It is not easy to give such a name to a being. I think I remember recoiling with fear when the name came forward to take up position. A Tomb(e) which erects itself. But I was thirty-three years old. It is generally about the age of twenty-two that a general, says Stendhal, has the greatest ability to make up his mind in two minutes over what is most at stake in a battle. And it is about the age of thirty-three that an 'author' makes up his mind to look Tombe in the face and side-on.

Tombe! is an imperative proper noun.

As *tumba*, it calls for the fall but it can be hurled upwards. Besides, at the origin, at the Greek then Latin

2

root, *tombe* is a tumulus which swells, comes up and rises. Like the seed of being, which interrupts its germination in the over-dry atmosphere of Proust's sickroom, which is dead and which resurrects as soon as he reads an author whose cry he recognizes. Such as the hooting of the tawny owl for Chateaubriand, the one who was writing his memoirs from Beyond the Grave, sitting in his coffin.

Tombe has a tubercular root. The stone covers itself with plants. Memory grows again beneath the oblivion which buries it.

As *tumber*, it was the cry of jugglers, of whirlers and dancers who acrobat between life and death. There is some squirrel in *Tombe*.

I had completely forgotten, lost, unvisited this Tombe, this book, in accordance with the fate and the tradition of the theme of the grave in my life.

Luckily, I had just got back to tomb, as one gets back to earth, the tomb of my father, that is to say, my father fallen to his grave and raised [*tombé et relevé*] at the Saint-Eugène cemetery in Algiers, in Spring 2006, when René offered to bring out *Tombe* again. I note that René has the incalculable advantage of advancing under the protection of such a given name, especially when dealing with somebody like me, on whom the signifier leaves a strong impression and imprint. To resurrect *Tombe*!

All the tombs of my life were born from the Tomb of my father. Never seen the Tomb again for fifty years.

In 2007 I had never reread *Tombe*. This book shares the fate of some of the books which scare me. They seem to me to contain or hold secrets or that beings remain in secret in them. As if I were afraid of death or of the dead. Or worse still: as if I feared to discover that the thing, or the dreaded being, is not dead. But that some *late fire* [feu] smoulders beneath the ashes [*cendre*].[3] These disturbing books lead their silence and their presence in my library behind my back under those very strong names which they possess. I consciously hold them at a distance. Topping the list of these threateners is *Le Prénom de Dieu*, the book from before all my books. The Predecessor. It is also the first 'book'—the first feared 'Thing', which came to me as if from some uncanny part of myself, the messenger of uncontrollable powers which prowl in our depths—and it was also the proof frightening me that I had perhaps fallen into follyterature [*folittérature*]. This *Prénom de Dieu*, which was tremblingly whispered to Jacques Derrida and was for him inaugural and indelible as a blow. He called it the *ulo* [olni] (unidentified literary object). One day in 1998, he rereads it and talks to me about it again at length. I fled. I wanted to know nothing of it. 'You

---

3 A reference to Jacques Derrida's *Feu la cendre*, whose title likewise plays on the two meanings of *feu*. [Trans.]

know everything's in it . . .' he said. 'No, no, I know nothing.' And I held by this, and I hold by this. *Tombe* has inherited from *Le Prénom de Dieu*. These are explosive 'Things', with a timing device.

On that 15 August 2007, I reread *Tombe*. An incredibly living grave. I could not do otherwise. I am writing these lines on 30 August. I forget, I am forgetting. Tomb, book, scissors, unconscious: it opens and closes.

NB. I have never returned to *Tombe*. *Tombe* returned. Tombe leaves again. Tombe is animated by the spirit of revenants.

There was the first step of a return one night, between two continents, a who goes there? murmured from afar by Frédéric-Yves Jeannet. 'What is this thing, Tombe?' he wrote to me, where one finds

> *Dioniris Adonis Peruvia Pergamum Persephony hence will to novel* [volonté de roman] *and circulation of myths (it is by way of a roundabout allusion to come '. . . he compares her to a snake with several mouths to his own heart turned against him to a Mexican sacrifice in which he would be the priest the heart the wrenching of the heart . . . ,' p. 145). There is of course an Egyptian side in this personal mythology with the bond: death of Dioniris— arrived in Peruvia—the destiny and the pen—and what is veiled . . . the ripped paper, the pen and our bedsheets (p. 153), work of embalming the*

mummy, the undone wrappings, themes which will be found again and developed in La, *and one also finds*: 'Tombe *is but a faint emanation of the book of books'* (*p. 154*), '*We shall write the book which is beyond the book*' (*p. 157*), *etc. It is also a first great travel book, before the* '*Book of the Dead Women*' *which* La *also is.*

said, from his Occident, the reader who dreams my texts more strongly than me.

Then I had said:

The book of books, the book towards which I go, still in the one which I am writing, scurries off in front of me, like the sacred animal which makes all impure knights run towards mortal purity [. . .] Sometimes this pursuit, begun straightaway, already *Dedans*, already *Tombe*, tires me so much that often I feel like dying = sleeping. Dreaming perhaps that I write it, at last?

In 1968/69, I wanted to die, that is to say, stop living, being killed, but it was blocked on all sides.

I began dreaming of writing a Tomb(e) for myself. This would be a testament. The word 'testament' in my tradition, that of Shakespeare and German Romanticism, is *spirited* [fait de l'esprit]. It has Wit or *Witz* in German. Sounding like *vite* (quick) in French. It has quick wits [*fait vite*]. Wit or *Witz* quickly yields *vite* and

6

therefore *Vif* (lively). It goes too quickly to be stopped. This is why, in this literary tradition of mine, in which word and wit are allied, the word 'testament' quickly [*a vite fait*] turns into a witty *textamant*.

Textamants (all of Stendhal, for instance) are books heading straight to perdition. Hence the rhythms, which are changed as often as the post changes horses, full rein [*bride abattue*], ellipses, imperative presents of swiftness, shortcuts

As if speed [*vitesse*]—and the *wittext*[4]—had to compensate for the brevity of life. Not to allow a second of the Time-which-remains to be lost.

The word is madly active. The sentence is mine-blowing [*fait mine*]. A gold mine.

There are sentences deep as lovers' beds. Sentences which are epoch-making, keys, books of magic spells, philosophy treatises.

Haste, speed, principles of my writing, as of those I love. And Swift [*Vite*] does not mean short—but make haste, run and think. For thought is very swift, swifter than itself, in order to cover distances beyond the known.

Haste me to know't, that I, with
wings as swift / As meditation of the thoughts
of love / May sweep to my revenge
(*Hamlet* I.5.29)

---

4 In English in the original. [Trans.]

Swift, like feverish Hamlet who makes haste and hastens so many others, in the five-act-long tumult. *Tumult*, which sounds like a sibling of *Tombe*.

When I was writing *Tombe* in 1970 I wanted to raise a tomb [*relever une tombe*], and recover from [*relever de*] a poisonous death. I wanted to disinter a secret and I interred [*enfouissais*] it beneath a text. I worked nonstop, I burrowed [*fouissais*], *Tombe* worked mole-like. Curiously the squirrel, in some cases, also works mole-like. Thus the Squirrel in *Tombe*, an American citizen also (I will speak about this below), is half an under-earthling [*souterrien*]. *Tombe* wanted still to come out alive from a sojourn in the Underworld and could not find the exit. The front door denies the way out. Another door must be found. *Tombe* must have begun clearing a text for itself beneath the text as early as 1964 in the USA. I could see the texts denting before my pages. Until one day when there was a rift in my lives through which *Tombe* was able to rise [*lever*]. But just this [*ce*] *Tombe* or that [*cette*] *tomb*. It's not that. I wanted to write a book, my tongue slipped and forked [*a fourché*], *Tombe* was born of this fork. Born forked. Double. With death as a third party [*en tiers*]. *Tombe* belongs in my work in general to the species of Books which run away; as soon as I try to write this book, it scurries off in front of me. Perhaps it's me who flees. Between us there is flight.

Tombe senses in advance, writes in advance the book which haunts it, unknowingly. Keeps watch. Waits. Unbeknownst to me. Waits thirty years. In 2001, the stage of *Tombe* opens onto *Manhattan, Lettres de la Préhistoire*. The Underworld has long been travelling.

It may not show at first glance but *Tombe* and *Manhattan* are *contratemporaneous 'twins'*.

The same goes for *Neutre*, which will have been *the prefigure* of *Le Jour où je n'étais pas là*.

Tombe would be the genogram of an incalculable lineage of books whose matrix can only be a *Peruvia*.

1970 *Tombe-Manhattan* 2001, it is as if I had laid siege to a Troy without succeeding in making it fall. Or walked round Jericho for the eighth time. But there are no trumpets, the trumpets are soundless, and telephones are made to be cut off.

Thirty years: *Tombe-Manhattan* testifies to the battle which is fought round the stronghold of a secret. This battle is the movement of literature itself. It is fuelled by a furious mixture of desire and resistance.

The desire to say everything and also not to say. One crawls in the straits of the unavowable. Between us is a fight: one of us must write what I cannot write, not look in the face even through writing, even with crooked writing [*de travers*]. The book comes out victorious but I don't. Somebody says to himself that a writer is like a general who wants to write a certain play, a certain book, and which the book itself, with the unexpected resources it reveals here, the dead end it throws up there, causes to deviate extremely from the preconceived plan. But this is not what I meant to say, says Saint-Loup. I said, says the new Saint-Loup: A general is like a writer. It's not at all the same thing. The secret of victory is *in diversion*. For a book to carry the day, the main desire must end in failure and diversion must succeed beyond all hope. But for that, diversion must succeed by itself. I cannot control it. If I made calculations, it would become the main operation.

Fall [*Tombe*], I said to myself.

'I fell with Nap.' Thus did Stendhal become the brilliant author of *Henry Brulard*.

During all these times, I wanted to *make the narrative* [récit] at all costs just as Saint Augustine says that he wanted to *make truth*. This is precisely what I could not do. I called this phantom text *Le Récit*. I pursued it relentlessly. Better die than give up the chase. The radical difference with Captain Ahab: If I had been able to find my White Sperm Whale [*mon Baleine Blanc*], which hides in the belly of the world with its denizen under the name of Jonas, I would have loved him. Too late would not have been too late. Each time I began again, as one does with fishing, the book on the run before me bore [*porte*] the transitional name *Le Récit*.

When I write *Manhattan, Lettres de la Préhistoire*, in 2001, it is the ninth time I'm having a go at the fortress of this narrative, this book which eludes me for as soon as I come near it irresistibly I flee from it. As it remains, so strong in the spectre-filled half-light, and I have been catching a glimpse of it for decades without ever being able to grasp its features, its face, its name—one may say that the struggle between Jacob and the angel starts again—I name it by the most vague antonomasia: Le Récit. A real reef [*récif*]. I crash against it ten times. But when at last, in an ultimate moment of wild embrace, I know how to make it say *Manhattan*, that's its name, I do not turn back one second towards *Tombe* which I am aware is one of its Precedents. Absolutely not. Knowing all too well that I would fall into it, as fore-told. *Manhattan, Lettres de la Préhistoire* has a prehistory, and before this prehistory is another prehistory. One thus goes back from scar to scar, along a ladder of lesions, towards a lost originary trauma.

The story which remains 'the first' and which took place in reality 'in reality', the one which makes a remain-der—a trace—and whose smallest chapters are archived in the memory of Leviathan-*Manhattan*, was much more powerful in reality than reality. It was incredible, at each minute. I consigned it only once, naked, that is to say, as wholly naked as possible, at least what I could see of it through the cracks of blindness. It was in 1965, in the end, I exposed it to Jacques Derrida, the exposition lasted for hours for it seemed to me that I had to deploy exactly the whole tissue of truths. I exposed it as in the Bible one exposes a child sentenced to death to the chance of a river. That can take place only once. And soon afterwards Oblivion begins.

As a crypt, *Tombe* contains specific points and details which I myself have forgotten.

When I say this is a tissue of truths, I speak 'the truth' about truths. All that is written is somehow true. There is a story. All this becomes truer and truer with time. 'A tissue of truths' has the power to bring back to life the catachresis which lies beneath a tissue of lies. What truths and lies have in common is the tissue. Catachresis is a weird figure. It is as cliché as can be but it makes itself conspicuous as an oral spy within the institution of literature. Sometimes Tombe speaks 'modern' like my mother.

Haunting fears of Tombe. *Tombe* is haunted. Haunted is Tombe by all the other tombs. A tomb wanders. I try to cover it with kisses, with tears, with ivies. It dashes off.

The singularity of this Tomb(e) is that it is a Phantom Tomb. I am speaking of the Tomb(e) of the book, in the book, the tomb which the main character expects, Dioniris, Phantom of Tomb(e)

A Tomb(e) which will not take place—in reality

12

A Tomb(e) which will have taken place as a fantasy. There is therefore no(t) more Tomb(e).

My Phantom Tomb(e)s: it's my tradition

Lost, fallen graves [*Tombes tombées*], tombs entombed for real. Tomb of my German grandfather Michael Klein fallen to his grave on the Russian front in 1916, spotted last in a Byelorussian forest. Tomb of my son vanished in the limbo of a wall in Algiers. Tomb of my father kept lost in Algeria. Tombs of Orphans. Tomb of Orpheus which cannot be found. Naturally, one draws gold galore [*on fait de l'or*] from this perdition.

But in *Tombe* the mad lovers' bed opens up. A love bed arguably always leaves room for death.

Antony and Cleopatra never stop dying for one dies a lot and often before the end. At least ten times. As soon as there is Love enters Death. Death makes its nest in love. Everywhere, in any literature, in any reality, there are always two of us plus Death. Death as a plus, as a witness. It is as if 'iloveyou' had as a synonym 'we're going to die.' One of us will outlive the other. And he will die from this survival.

Here the particular feature is that death is not called for by love, it's the former that calls for the latter. In the beginning there is the end. Love arises out of fear—over, under death.

I love you because you are going to die. No, it's not that, *I* do not love you: *I cannot but* love you and mourn you. You still live but already I mourn you. He the pages, I the sails/veils [*voiles*]. He weaves the pages, I cram on sails/put on veils [*mets les voiles*]. He the breath, I the fright.

Love's bitter mystery: if Love were Death it would have looked like it. The terrible fate of too-handsome Adonis.

> It is often when I am most sick, when I have no ideas left in my head nor any strengths left, that this ego which I sometimes recognize catches sight of the links between two ideas, just as it is often in autumn, when there are no more flowers or leaves, that one senses the most profound harmonies in landscapes. And this boy who thus plays in me on the ruins needs no food, he merely feeds on the pleasure afforded him by the vision of the idea he discovers, he creates it, it creates him, he dies, but an idea resurrects him, like those seeds which stop germinating in too dry an atmosphere and which are dead: but a little humidity and warmth is enough to resurrect them.[5]

When in 2007 I read these notes on literature and criticism by Proust, I discover the germ of Gold for

---

5 Marcel Proust, 'Notes sur la littérature et la critique' in *Contre Sainte-Beuve*, p. 303. Cixous quotes this very passage in *Philippines* (Laurent Milesi trans.) (Cambridge: Polity, 2011), pp. 34–5, which we are reproducing here in our translation. [Trans.]

Tombe. In 1970, the boy who plays in me on the ruins creates, dies, resurrects; I call him Dioniris. His double is Adonis.

All the lovers who play on the ruins of the sex of Gold, who are one body with the lyre, and of their bodies make the book, are related to Dioniris. They haunt the memory of this text.

Dioniris,

The character in *Tombe*—only one has the honour of the name—is related to this marvellous Adonis loved beneath the earth by Persephone and on earth by Venus, then beneath the text by the Shakespeare who plays the roles of *Venus and Adonis.* Its immense legend lingers on in the East (in Lebanon as well as in Syria, in Greece and in Palestine) as well as in the West. From one text to the other, from one edge to the other, from one letter to the other from one language to the other, Adonis is also Lord Adonai. His being is garlanded with a vegetation[6] which mimics naturally the several stages of his

---

6 Several flower legends are linked to the story of Adonis; not only the mythical origin of myrrh (Myrrha's tears) but also of the rose. At the origin, the rose used to be white but, as she was rushing to the rescue of her wounded friend, Aphrodite pricked her foot on a thorn and the colour of her blood coloured the flowers which are consecrated to her. Anemones, too, were supposedly born from the blood of wounded Adonis . . . The goddess shed as many tears as Adonis spilled drops of blood; of each tear a rose was born, of each drop of blood an anemone.

fate. The text runs its course, it leaves narration, it dies, it resurrects. Love and death contend for it. As in life. As in books. Its path is closely lined with myrrh and thorns, with mint and demented women [*de menthe et de démentes*]. Long after, after many books and deaths, I go to Algiers, in 2006, I find the Tomb of Tombs again, my father's grave, which is also the grave and the cradle of Tombs which are the secret-filled chests of my books, dreaming beneath a cypress. The cypress is also a god in India. We are metonymies, we cling, vivacious mortals that we are, like ivies to the banks of shipwrecked books.

Dioniris is born returning like a revenant. He returns from before *Tombe* and from after *Tombe*, a phantom which contends for *Portrait du Soleil* with Dieubis, another Lord who also signs his texts.

In honour of her friend, Aphrodite founded a funeral festival which Syrian women celebrated each year in spring. Seeds were planted in vases, crates, etc., which were watered with warm water in order to make them grow very quickly. These plantations were called 'Adonis' gardens'. Plants thus forcefully grown soon died after coming out of the ground, symbolizing Adonis' fate. And the women let out their ritual whining over the fate of the young man loved by Aphrodite. The Semitic origins of this legend are obvious; the god's very name can be traced back to the Hebrew word meaning 'Lord'. The cult of Adonis spread in the Mediterranean world during the Hellenistic age and its legend is already represented on Etruscan mirrors (taken from Pierre Grimal's *Dictionnaire de la Mythologie*).

'Only he should write my books, the boy who plays in me on the ruins, the ruin player,' Proust thinks. The musician who ruins. He would also play with the word Ruin, he could unite or ruin, sense the Dioneiric book waking up between two ideas ...

> [. . .] movement of the book fallen from the sky, blessed, but blessed as one blesses the dugout of the dead by sending it to the other bank, to Peruvia where the father lives [*vit le père*], on a journey, before again sitting down at his table in front of another grave, and thus thirty-four years later *Si près* will close on a *looping* round a grave where one sheds the tears of the book just delivered and yet always still to be written

says Frédéric-Yves Jeannet to me on 1 January 2008.

South of Manhattan, between East Village and West Village, is where the Garden of Disappearances lies hidden eternally, that is to say Washington Square. Peruvia stretches all round this heart watched over by the tribes of squirrels. The entrance to my first literary infernos can be found on MacDougall Street, at the corner of Bleecker Street. Naturally, before coming to Washington Square, I had already been, literally, in a book, to *Washington Square*. And before that I had already known the Jardin d'Essai in Algiers.

The Garden of Disappearances? There is always one, a Garden where Disappearances appear, that is to say, disappearances in the process of happening, before our eyes, scared, powerless to interrupt the disappearancing. One *sees disappearing*. That lasts a few moment during which life turns itself into death whereas life and death keep up the misunderstanding, the equivocation. Are we still? Are we already? It seems to me I have already-been-there. There is dream in the air. Washington Square was my first Garden of 'Alreadyseens' which make texts rise. On this American Journey, I had my eyes open, yet it seemed to me that I was in a dream. Or in a still unwritten book. I was at Caffe Reggio. I was reading Milton's *Lycidas* while waiting for him. I was speaking in American. It so happens that I wrote my first strange pages in American. I could equally have been in Pompeii in 79, near the Forum. I went to the Village Voice with the beloved. Reality was a dream.

Literary America is that of Kafka: an *Amerika* truer than reality, where the character manages to arrive only by losing his way. There is something bewitching in 'America' for the European, said Kafka, who arrives in New York like Ulysses at the Sirens'. However tightly one blocks one's ears, one hears the Voices. Now these are the Voices of the myth, the most ancient and charming, the most seductive voices. Come and play with me! Come and die with me!

America disguises itself as the USA. As a great usurious power. As problems. I have always loved the States

[*Étazuni*]. In the USA I have always been terrorized. Perhaps I have always loved being terrorized. Or else I have been terrorized from loving. In 1969 or 70, I was so afraid of burning myself again at the Stakes of Thorns that I would not have said the name even. This is why this story happens in Peruvia. Literature is such an Eldorado [*Pérou*], is it not?

My States, that is to say, Manhattan and surroundings have been Libraries. Cities of Books. I went to the cafes in the Village as in books. The books were high and trembling like skyscrapers. When I was reading *Samson Agonistes*, I could see Samson shaking the columns of the philistine Temple while weeping his last pains away; that was on 5th Avenue. Before, I had been to Caffe Reggio, and I had read Paul Celan in English in 1964 on worn velvet seats nowadays in 2007 I still read Paul Celan at the Reggio as at the Strada di Mercurio in Pompeii waiting for the sun.

What remains of American immensity in *Tombe* is mythical immensity. One could be nothing but gods mowed down by wild boars in those streets. The gods who neither are nor are not. Likewise, when I read Ovid, whether the *Metamorphoses* or *Tristia*, Greece or Rome happen in America. The music is by Mahler or else Thelonious Monk.

It occurs to me that all the evil which I have known in New York, where the first great performance of follyterature took place, has turned into fecundity on the mode of the *Metamorphoses*.

The Squirrel has always been there.

All my work has been presigned by the *Squirrel on Washington Square*. The Squirrel comes from the depths of my memory, already when I was five and before this already, before my memory. I think that the Squirrel is also somebody. He is somebody. And not just anybody. If *Tombe* were to have a subtitle, it would be *Life or Death of a Squirrel*. I will never forget this 1964 squirrel. I did not know, during a piercing time, if it was alive or dead, inside or outside, I took him for a sign. It is as if he were the real allegory of my whole death agony. What *is* this being which gives or takes or gives back or loses life or death? I do not know.

A half-buried squirrel has heralded and inaugurated the menagerie of all my books. And all the half-way beings of which one does not know whether they are going or returning.

The Squirrel or Adonis, Lord of the texts, will have resurrected once more in the text called *Ciguë* (Hemlock) in order to celebrate a new agony, solitary and bloody, of himself.

It all started transforming from and because of a Squirrel on Washington Square, my life changing into literature unbeknownst to me this October morning of 1964 from one moment to the next: I had really thought it was dead. I bend over. I tremble. Straight afterwards, a leap . . . resurrection. Then from death to resurrection, from book to book, from literature to reality, I have never inaugurated a notebook without a greeting from the squirrel, to the squirrel and so on. Later, it reappears under the guise of *Goya's Half-Dog*. Still rather lively than dead or rather: rather than dead, always still alive. But one day, when my brother calls me on the telephone, saying to me: 'Sit down,' I understand that, this time, 'it' is totally dead. My brother found it dead on my bed. I beg my brother: Bury it. He does not say no.

And for the first time it was over.

'Sit down,' says my brother's voice, that meant 'so that you don't fall'. I never spoke to him about the Squirrel. He has never read *Tombe*. If he had, that would not have lifted the secret. Even I did not know the subterranean geography of the kingdom of the Squirrel.

One walks alive, from one second to the next it's death, Washington Square a cemetery; I tottered, seeing the corpse of a squirrel half buried in the ground, as if it had tried quickly to conceal its death in the Underworld, but, caught out and struck as it goes down, it remains frozen like an inhabitant from Herculanum, 'it's art's secret' my friend the American poet has said; I tottered, seeing in the half-body of the corpse the annunciation of the fate of my friend the dying poet. I saw two deaths [*vis deux morts*]. I know it, vainly I fear it, since Washington Square, I've lived off deaths [*vis de morts*]. 'Submission at the book's door,' says my friend. 'Go past death, and it's literature. Go beneath the earth, follow the squirrel, it leads you to the root of secrets.'

I have not been able to accomplish this narrative for four years. Four years ago I said 'Bury it.' I said 'Swear.' I said 'Have you done it?' 'How do you want me to?' 'Swear! Swear.' 'I swear. OK, I'm going.' 'Come back.' 'I'm going.' 'Where do you want?' 'Beneath a pine tree. Religiously.'

I'm leaving it at that.

Of all my revenants The Squirrel is literarily the most revenant, the most literary of my revenants. I could not say to my brother, 'Here you're burying my most ancient god, my religion, the most abandoned of my prophets, the last of the Mohicans, the Incarnation of the Genius of Literature, the Gambler [*Joueur*] of Fatalities, the thwarter [*déjoueur*] of verdicts, you're burying in this little hole several continents and four graves, it's The City you're burying, The City of Returns [*à Revenirs*], the first and last cradle, you're burying the adorable mistake of truth, from today onwards there will be no more Resurrections in Reality they will henceforth resurrect in the dream world.'

I see, today, this summer of 2007, that already the notebooks, the letters, are laid out *within* the text which they gather. All the supports and subjectiles on which the general text of my books stretches and interweaves and which are props on stage, have become, since so long ago, *Witnesses. Tombe* is a book which runs its course and not mine. I open, I enter, and I see that *Tombe* speaks about *Tombe* in *Tombe* and more subtly than the author would know how to. It is not the first time that I will have been surpassed by the Subject.

The Book is itself a character of the book. I can see the Book young, just as I can see myself young in a dream

The knowledgeable reader—who I was not—could have spoken of *Tombe* as a sort of metalepsis. I like the word, I take it, I can see that *Tombe* does speak from within the book on the book. The after-book comes before the book. The Tombe metalepsis is a manipulation on the play before–after. All this story is visibly affected by what is called the aftereffect [*après-coup*].

I admit: I write books which quickly gain the upper hand. They are like the characters whom the playwright, as soon as these beings have 'set', sees drifting away, deciding on the action and doing only just as they please.

If I'd had other eyes to read him I could have reproduced his secret ink and *Tombe* would not have lacked the book in the place of which this one is being written. But if I had known why *Tombe* is being written and not the other one, I would not have had the desire or the obligation to return to this wall to the point of delirium.

23

All the delusions and all the cautions and all the wiles of conservation had settled there.

That's why this book here lacks the book of death, which this book is only a parody of. But this book does not come far from the book of death, and at times brushes against it.

That is how *Tombe* comes close to what, much later, I will eventually call The-Book-which-I-Do-Not-Write. This Book-which-I-Do-Not-Write is the all-powerful-other of all my books, it sparks them off, makes them run, it is their Messiah, and in my literary religion it is always promised-not-yet-come and it will come only one day after the last page of the last book in my lifetime.

Let's make no mistake about it: this strange, terrible story is not mine, others in other names have been subjected to it, and I had already read it a hundred times. That's why, having these readings, this memory, and this terror, I tried to divert its course and counter-write it

The universe is all metaphors and metamorphoses, as natural as when Ovid depicted the states of the soul in metamorphoses, that is to say, the soul always embodied, as natural as in the days of Shakespeare or Rimbaud, Mallarmé or Milton. Alteration is every-where. As is the case 'in reality', if reality, in its actuality dated from a cold [*froidie*], unpoetic epoch, does not refuse it. But we're living through a faceless epoch in which reflections are borrowed from glossy photo magazines.

When I read *A Life of Napoleon*, and I see Stendhal struggling, like a lion against the python about to devour it, joyous but always utterly lonely, against the hypocritization of contemporary society, I recognize him as the prophet of the shabby [*miteux*] incipient twenty-first century. Better, the reverse of Mythical. Shabby, narrow-minded and regressive, slipping way behind the daring abilities of the century of Freud, Benveniste, Derrida, Proust, Deleuze, Joyce, Gracq, of all the pioneers of language and fantasy who were not afraid of gods. In which they resurrected the mischievous folly of the Greeks and of the Bibles. In the street, in the metro at the *Lethe* station beneath Montparnasse, as in Phoenix Park in the city of Dublin, or in Central Park NY, one meets the dead ready to return, the sumptuous but too often lagged denizens of immortality, if one is not too timorous, the wrathful divinities of the telephone, the whole people of the mythological worlds. Should one take a walk one fine morning on these Elysian Fields, one will come across Venus, Adonis, Albertine, Fabrice, Brulard, Dedalus, Socrates, Achilles, Penthesilea, the Marquise of O. And all these poets thinkers of the subject in language, of metamorphosis and mobility, all decipherers of the dual heritage, heirs of the pasts and inventors of futures to come, all the sages, the faithful, the hospitallers who welcome in their texts and relaunch the precedents in the descendants, they testify and show that literature is erudite and philological right into its most familiar forms, that it is excavation and cathedral, labyrinth, calculation, geometry and virgin forest, theatre to the very last words, that it has read seen tasted forgotten it all and found it again, that it is planet and meteor, layered expanse and landing strip for still unidentified events.

Tombe could be mistaken for a new edition of *Venus and Adonis*. In reality, I saw Venus and Adonis in 1964 starting again on their run against the cruel flow of time, accompanied by Death which does not care a whit about our trembling fits, in the thickets of Central Park. They sometimes stayed in a secret hotel in Manhattan. In 1964 as in 1592 in Homeria as in America.

★

In the thick of life, the premonition of death comes to our minds. Not only to our minds: to our hearts, our lungs, our throats. This pitiless thought, the Anticipator, the one which spends its time making advances to death, is without pity for me, without pity for us.

I do not know—how—to die—not to die—how not to betray. How one is—in the paroxystic experience of mystery—an accomplice to disaster. One commits suicide according to the mode described by Kafka: I see the rope to hang somebody in the courtyard, I think it is waiting only for me, I go there. One expects death. I throw myself to the rope, to the neck of Death. However much I read Montaigne, nothing doing. Nobody learns how to die. The Event lands [*tombe*] upon us. The hourless Event. The volcanic Event which lifts our floors, blows off our roofs, scratches out our eyelids, disarticulates us, throws us into convulsions. I have nothing to do with it and it is all my fault. One should not think about it. It is *always too early* to think about Death.

The curtain raised one minute too early, what can one see? What can one see? Who is death? This woman,[7] the Apparent, the worrying vulgar beautiful relative [*parente*], impressive like all that outside waits before the door. If I had been able to kill her! but precisely it was impossible to kill her: to notice her is to give her back life. What seems to have to remain hidden must remain hidden behind the silk of the curtain, but those who out of awkwardness or by chance have disturbed that which is bound [*se lie*] from behind to the invisible, that which can be read [*se lit*] behind the back of the book, those see death *one minute too early* but they cannot be dead and they are thrown back onto the silk. They see what is in store for them, there is no time left at all

---

7 Death (*la mort*) is of feminine gender in French and therefore, unlike in English, symbolized as a woman. [Trans.]

In the end, death leaves me and now I am thrown into a time which is not a piece of time but which is made of an extra-temporal substance.

The tomb is my magical flagstone, my uneven cobblestone. One foot on the higher cobblestone, I go back in the past until now.

When I think that my friend J. D. claims at the beginning of his book *H. C. for Life, That Is to Say . . .* that 'Hélène Cixous took sides "for life".'

'Yet he had read *Tombe*?' 'Yes, as with all the other texts—as the first reader.' And yet. It means therefore that *Tombe* is on the '*side of life against death, for life without death, beyond a death whose test and threat are none the less endured, in mourning even in the life blood and breath, in the soul of writing*'.[8]

On the side of life unto the Tomb(e).

---

8 Jacques Derrida, *H. C. for Life, That Is to Say . . .* (Laurent Milesi and Stefan Herbrechter trans and annot.) (Stanford: Stanford University Press, 2006), p. *xiii*. [Trans.]

Tomb(e)

Impassive

I swim far from here, between two thousand rocks and
there are no waters

Him! Who else but Him! impassive there porphyry
Light is not so bright The earth all around rolled up in
the storm's sheet is nothing more than the tain of the
mirror which reflects the blinding splendour of Him

Do you see something? Nothing. One guesses only.

Outside ordinary lands, where the seas
, leaving their beds flowed into the Osseant
, where stars and winds rage and throw in disarray
, where science is a dream of natural laws
, the Sex of Gold [*d' Or*]★ stands up erect by itself.

This famous monument vestige of creation gives itself in its infinite duplicity to be seen by the loving who have not been afraid of taking themselves for gods. —Gods are men without eyes—. It is away from eyes or under shelter that the Sex of Gold rises by itself nobody manages to reach it who still clings to water or the mirror's gaze. Love, whose sextant it is, checks the beings it attracts in the way in which the loving magnet sun [*nous aimantant*]★ controls us and keeps pulling the wool over our virgin eyes

The Sex of Gold is used to measure the level of immortality in the lovers' desire   OF

1 At that time my name was his name   O
was *Dioniris* I think but his natural name was   N
the one which served indifferently for him   E
or me was
Orphan, incomparable, damp garden   O
Red Three times more beautiful than me   R

2 My name is heart-rending, it was tearing me apart, on his moist lips

3 What was Achilles' age for Love and what age for death the same age and what age was Dioniris for me the same age as Achilles for Penthesilea's love, thus sometimes one of us was thirty years old then the other was three and sometimes twenty and the other thirteen and sometimes sixteen and seventeen or eighteen and

fifteen or twenty-eight and five or everything together
one, two, four, nine, seventeen, in very little time, and
we protruded and turned back from one body to the
other, children, adolescents, birds, jealous, spasmodic,
without ever wounding our sole memory whose tissues
were as supple as the neck of a womb

4 Afterwards . . .

THE OTHER EDGE

. . . His death like a bad joke I haven't said anything yet.

5 I haven't (. . afterwards . . .) opened these warm dry lips
yet

6 I don't know how to forget, I know that all that is
unforgettable can be forgotten between high and low,
in particular
your death, but it takes place thus where waters cover
the trenches,
Now, where I swim between two thousand rocks, there
are no waters and the rocks chisel my body and
flush it crimson

7 I haven't opened my mouth yet (chest of the twice
born) which is now useless. If one opened it

8 One would see his dead dark-coloured tongue
Expired swollen motionless decomposed

9 Useless

10 I was sucking away at it and chewing it when

11 My name was his name

12 His slightly salty taste, now just the envelope of this
taste—his name of sperm salt and amomum, his
truth—moves me deeply, irrupts me
I don't see it, I don't taste it, I smell it
Infallibly
13
Its smell: recognizable among ten thousand
The smell of Lovely Mint [*la menthe*]★

14 Yet I am wary of myself like the plague, just as death
must be wary of life, just as Love must be wary of death
and
Of bitter plants from down below and since Seduction
flees from itself
Life is in the bag—life: the story. The bag:
15 a simple pocket, one squeezes it tight with cords. (Similar to the sex of the loving woman [*aimante*]★ into
which he would have introduced for fun before
making love a leaf ripped out of a schoolboy's notebook). The bag, or cage, or chest

Then, what is being written

Do I want what I want yes no or all
And so on do I want all   OR
16 That which I wanted that which I want is   OR

    A nothing which is beyond the whole and

When I write my tongue is invisible. My mouth is
17 blind It's normal: the eye is in the mouth is in crimson
It's the tip of the tongue whose end one can never see
When I laugh I feel it throbbing: it hears. But it's rare.

    (*squirrel*)

An immense grief pleases me, consoles me
18 —Once more lament yourself, once again—Plays death
to me

    Sets in motion

19 That would be the story whose periphery would be
time and each sentence of which one of the worlds. It
would take place in Peruvla whose capital Pergamum
is moved by a thousand sails. It would be red-coloured,
sometimes perse [*pers*]★, sometimes at the vanishing
point, white as a fable. This story would not wake up
but it would be lifted, overthrown, turned topsy-turvy
with such violence that the sails would be thrown up
the masts wrecked the rigging broken within the lands

which themselves would be fractured, only the Sex of
Gold would be immutable

All of it

20 HE, (*Dioniris*), the one who says: 'I've told you all.'
When we're ninety years old . . . Then the land will be
remodelled
21 I will be out, I will have seen, I will have lost or I will
be other or something close and without eyes
22 (Just before his death) I was getting ready to go out
Dioniris said: 'Remember.'
I retrace my steps running, I had
perhaps already forgotten,   the smell
already been forgotten; all will have   of
already changed; I ran;   lovely mint
In the meantime: all has changed. And once more

(or Adonis)

I could hear myself repeating: 'What a story, what a
23 story
And nobody wants to tell it to anybody!' All of a sudden after all
it had become the story . . .

On which face or skin

It's impossible to say: when we're ninety years old

24 yet it's possible to write it, now [*or*]★
This will never happen, we'll never be that
For the source of sperm has run dry

Is liquid or congealed

Yet without this sentence how would we exist,
25 without these broken
sentences which already survive me already bury me
or drown me or cuddle me less dead but less vibrant
than men who live and die
more than any of them free but corruptible

or tanned

The whole universe in its shell would be balanced on
26 a speck of dust
more securely than our bed keeping itself on the edge
of disappearance:
in this disastrous time the slightest gesture had incalculable effects on destiny,
at the same time destiny had the fineness of dust

$\overset{t}{S}\underset{c}{\text{-rolling}}$ [Par chemin]★ *by air or land*

So necessary was it to be naked that we found it very
hard to clothe ourselves. There was a blouse, some
distance from my body.

37

It was impossible to fasten the neck. The folds of the blouse floated bulged scattered round the neckline.

Impossible to gather the neck, I could not find any cord nowhere, the folds were receding, the fever rose, I was sweating with symbolic anguish, I was secretly rejoicing over the resistance

of the tissue, I was marvelling or getting frightened about meeting the obscure forces and the wiliness of immortality, I was twisting my neck

    impossible

(Thinking of the ways in which the dead can think and of what they think about being dead thinking themselves dead I was digging in the

rash stubborn absent-minded manner of another than oneself so much and so absent-mindedly that suddenly the

membrane burst open and hurled was my soul among the dead where nothing is thought)

27 The impossible is the
    possible OTHER
    takes after THE ONE

    Quite similar among the unbridled gathers,
    The tissue embroidered with stealth
    Stormy, barely held at the magnetic shoulderpoles,

(It was a traditional blouse woven of those transparent creaseproof veils always creased as if by pressing hands) To my perse phantom

On which Pergamum skin?

28 On the white veils of the blouse danced the thousands of white signs drawn with a needle, coloured, precise, pressed in echoes and mends, the dry scratched creased shimmering white tearing its own texture with its glare so dazzling that their minute syntax cannot manage to shine through to the eye. This gave me a joy like a fever, a fever, a precipitation, the mere sight of this albeit off-white, flickering linen made me feverish: impossible to fasten the blouse. My fingers sweaty from groping for the cords nervously threaded through at the neckline. Fuss as I might: no cord anywhere. Had there ever been any? Was it not presumptuous to believe that the model brings about the same reconstitution for ever? Perhaps it was an old cordless blouse which because it was cord-less got my threads in a twist because I was waiting, memory that I am, what should not be . . .

On which linen made gold

a bit asleep, still in bed, I had slipped on the blouse without getting out of bed, out of need, my fingers a bit asleep, a bit trembling, moist but steady, and trembling with excitement or fever and as if with joy,

because it seemed obvious to me that on this gesture
the following one depended, and on the following one
the following, and on the following my whole life up
to its way of dying and
the story
(I wanted to tie the cords anew. Groping, trembling,
not knowing.)

Comes the blind Fury

29 The Story of my fingers on fragrant tissues, running
around
that slender neck of mine, feverish, tingling, at my fingertips by heart the oldest older knowledge what I
know through the memory of fingers of a pink silk
dress hung very very high up in its self
in a dreamt wardrobe, and in a dream of a wardrobe an
almost colourless crepe-de-
Chine dress, flesh and skin, cut by Love, hung
long impalpable and the tissue ripens. I remember the
dress in crepe de Chine made to measure and I'd still
like today to put it on tomorrow. If only I'd put it on
wouldn't the wedding would it have taken place? I can
sense it its skin finer more elusive than my skin,

to the abhorred scissors

30 Isn't the most invisible the most dangerous? I don't
want to tie anew for the sake of renewing ties. Am I

not in bed between the fake pink linen sheets, directed towards the sun? To tell the truth, my intention was to tie the cords anew in order to untie them as one must do when one wants to ask the question of mortality. Or rather: How to untie what is not already tied? Then I would have folded my arms, lowered my eyes, grabbed the right and left sides of the blouse with opposite hands, unfolded my limbs, raised my arms stretched above my head wrapped in the veils, my body to my eyes: hidden. The head among the veils, in itself, arms twisted

to cleave through the fine carpet of life

31 To me the flesh to him the smell
To the Sex of Gold the smoke

32 I dreamt of Him last night, we were on the same vessel, a luxury vessel, of a foreign make, well kept, or rather: I had been in a somewhat old and sea-worn vessel I saw him steering one of those big imaginary mighty unobtainable sailing boats, but we were going nowhere. Dioniris and I and the others under other veils [*voiles*]★ we were going under sail [*voiles*]★. They circulated. I left mine. He put his away. Then we stood up next to each other, tall as towers, each desiring gently, with love, the other's immortality. Penthesilea Achilles.

Himself, through Himself with Himself

33 There where Hinnom becomes Gehenna and the dream its awakening I dreamt of Himself at night we were on the same foreign luxury vessel and I'd already done the same crossing. I saw him steering this big imaginary mighty sailing boat barely visible except in a dream. Dioniris I and others were going nowhere in a dream. Dioniris I and others under other veils we were going under sail naturally. They circulated. I let go of mine he put his away and we stood up next to each other tall as masts each desiring gently with love the other's immortality. The birds were fluttering about, the sailing boats were heaving, the masts were dancing, the waters were rushing and pushing us off.

We were staying at the top of a fabulous hotel set to deteriorate barely inaugurated already ruined the edifice was buffeted by the fiercest winds: on the left the wind of time was destroying the space it swept through. I stood away from the open window. I could see this wind harassing what was but a mush of air: hundreds of whirl-winds were swirling on themselves and ripping their own bellies open until they produced in the midst of their cruel movement a kind of lumpy icy blood. Dioniris Man thought it was merely a storm. I stood at the far end of the room and I was shouting for him to hear me, for the wind of time was screeching on my lips. The wind was swirling on itself at a high steady speed. Love had nested its fear right above my heart. It was fer-reting about, shaking itself abruptly like a squirrel near my ribs. The wind of time kills off. Millions of doors were banging. The fate of doors: to go with a bang. The fate of cords: to untie. I moved towards the east of the doomed hotel. I was frozen, my keenest desire was to burrow under some vast earth blanket with dark blue fringes whose warmth my body was inventing. I could catch sight of the land from the terrace, perhaps, the wind was there, I did not see the land: the waters had flowed back. The movement of waters was extraordinary: it was a joyous, nasty, horrible rising to be seen, the waters come from the horizon were unfurling from the extreme left to the horizon. They were yellow, rather heavy but young. Full of vigour, they clearly knew what they were breaking. They were swelling not the way seas do but by breaking and hurling the way mountains do. Vessels were flitting about and vanishing. Only one remained. I was frozen, without Dioniris, he was not where I was, tall as a tower and trembling with cold. I saw the yellow waters: they were neither thick nor deep but mineral almost of an incredible smoothness on huge broken rising surfaces. The invisible land was rolling below the tense yellow waters. I, standing, beside memory beside forgetting, dreaming amid my dreams with sails torn apart, my head elsewhere my body frozen.

There was one vessel left, with all its sails torn apart. I saw it gliding past over the big step of water which was moving from the west. Two men were left in the sailless hulk, what man could have escaped the big surging fit?

The two men stood at a right angle to the vertical step without flinching. I saw them walk very far from me very near very fast faces raised I saw their faces, one young, the other divine, and I recognized them as one recognizes oneself with uncertainty and without a doubt with the difference with indifference in the interstitial sky. I felt for them a big quiet familiar fear, fearless at bottom and bottomless but rising and melting and complacently unstable. The hotel was cracking plumb below the middle hall. The two men had come from the outermost reaches of history and were continuing on the Pacific bed. I, the pierced monument, the waters, the epicentre somewhere, in the East or in the West, otherless, the memory rising and newsless. The two men had looked too, their young divine faces astonished from being seen there, in this unexpected time, they being unexpected but always still expected, and I doubtless still unexpected.

(One day when he had said to me 'remember', no sooner had I taken three steps westward than I was seized with terror: What if already I was forgotten? If I had already forgotten? I retrace my steps running and running on his, and everything changed, and already he no longer is where he had been, I remember he had said 'Remember,' but I forgot, I forgot, I forgot or I didn't, how to know from now on and I was surrounded by memory.)

and the earth all around rolled up in the sheet wrung by the storm is now a mere tain of memory which reflects the astonishing splendour of Him.

I admire how the unsailed ship cleaves through the fringe of waters which fix its monstrous course and I fear. With a double face they move on, sure to arrive safe and sound. They do not seek help, it's in me on this throbbing pillar that fear tumbles down in overwhelming jolts like a squirrel's. From the horizon to the horizon an uninterrupted line closed and cleaving you'd believe nothing can streak the sea, always the same . . . impassive.

and I remember all that has not been:
how to tie anew what is not already tied, what is not already untied, how can what is tied be untied, how to tie what is already tied anew, for it is impossible to place what has never been, this is why my strength is lost, and my memory is higher than my story

And just as a vessel carried away by the wind's breath sees the lively harbour sink in, thus does life decline and sink before my eyes and I am carried away like what is loving by what is lovable

He loves the one who is the lover of beautiful things:

But have I really waited for him, had my waiting not always been the veil of my flight, had I not always already known wished dreaded refused hoped that my hope be dismissed, was I not sure when I called him by his proper noun that he had never had the ears which could hear that name

What does he love

And what will it be for the one to whom it will happen that beautiful things have become his? If he becomes mine, what will be of love and me?

THE HERB-AND-SPICE CRÊPE

... and how seduction flees from itself ...

It would be the story of Desire, each victory of which is a defeat and each defeat another victory. This story would recast loose lands and join ritually desiring fleshes, once again and once again and the edges of rivers being nearer the waters would spill onto a single bed thus and when the times were joined then eternity would rise. One must not leave out Lovely Mint, nor fire seeds, nor the spices that are suitable for the crêpe. If the crêpe rises, what is loosened may be joined, the sourmother [amère]★ flows into the semifather and man can look like woman just as gold can look like linen and linen gold and as the gold linen makes marriage a wild bed.

Far from cities and far from hotels and far from unwild lands not far from wild altars and not far from unwild lands it must be done one day or another neither here nor there in the crêpe nest not far from the destinal soil half way up almost outside ritually.

I see Dioniris' apparents the other day come straight from another time like those gods who are always somewhat looking at what we do. Dioniris crowned with roses and stars as it should be on my invisible breast floating cordless nowhere some distance away from the wild skin the blouse but colourless and not embroidered yet neither linen nor gold but of a skin-coloured crêpe around my naked shoulders. On either side are Dioniris' semifather and his sourmother. Whom does Dioniris please whom does he dazzle for which feast?

once more you Lovely Mint and once again brown myrtle and you ivy [lierre]★ *once again do lament for I am coming to wrench your harsh heads apart out of bitter constraint and costly affliction because Dioniris*

And now he is setting about making crêpes. You know that crêpe batter is a sign of marriage. It's the job of old women, I didn't pitch in to help with the batter, but I know it must be made, before the eye of the sourmother and before the eye of the semifather. And before mine. Have no doubt about its success. It all unfolds according to the book. Imagine what happens next and the three gazes hooked on the ordinary bowl. Mix the flours get to grips with the bowl prepare the

Aufhebung. There's an order, there are laws, there's a
system there's a conclusion: all this is exalting, symbolic
and divine. And the whole, first scattered in various
ingredients then homogeneous and desirable; all this
is satisfying. Immemorial crêpes, edible membranes,
melting emblems. If he's forgotten spices, sugar or
salt . . .

Why should the story come after four or a hundred
thousand years? And why is three next to two and next
to two why three and one? And what if three was next
to zero or one thousand one hundred?

and does the rite depend on crêpe or blouse, is it law
which makes marriage pass through flours and if I said
three next to one four five would that change the
course of History? And if Dioniris puts salt in the
beginning and sugar in the middle will the flours get
angry? In my place what would you have done in
Dioniris' place . . . now overtaken? Lifted? Worried
without worry yet worried overtaken by events: from
the bowl with mixed flours a hasty mountain rises
ineluctably yet is still held down at the bottom, I can
see it swelling and balancing the order of things: he's
also forgotten yeast. What can rise without yeast? Why
is there an order of ingredients and why the head over
the neck and the hands touching the arms? The semifather's eye follows the rising without batting an eyelid.
The sourmother keeps watch: Does Dioniris know
how to go about it? I don't doubt it: now still add salt

and sugar. The eye must outspeed the crêpe. If the crêpe is souffléed by its own puff and without yeast, then the question of the yeast must be thought through again. And therefore the question of writing? and of reading? and of all culture? So far Dioniris has not flinched. Only when the mountainous crêpe settles down by itself in the shape of a cone sliced down the middle and triggers off its own cooking does its heart abruptly explode in my breast; a terrifying pain which touches my body less than my eyes, but I want to see that. If the souffléed crêpe sets, cooked and golden, a crust already, is it still time to incorporate the yeast or will it have to be split open. Alas Dioniris' gestures . . . are slowed down, he's visibly suffering from distraction. The sourmother turns round in all directions. Let her do it, let her do it. The crêpe is delirious. Time is short. Desperate yet unfazed I now wish to flip the crêpe onto its raw side nervously on the verge of tears, proof that it's my life that is at stake here. I feel the need for the flip as if it had to do with my own past, I twist my muscles as I strive to reverse the sequence. Imagine that this crêpe is the substance of your life, how moved you would be to see it overspill its nature. Why put salt and sugar into a mountain which rises by itself? Solid, dry, fragrant, light, brittle, innocent. Is a saltless sugarless waterless milkless beerless and yeastless self-rising crêpe a real crêpe even if it is a fake crêpe and it is similar to a real crêpe? The sourmother comes to the rescue without any of the parties consenting, quick, she grabs a bottle of spices which she empties into the upturned bosom of the crêpe. Nobody is fooled: I sense and you sense and Dioniris knows how acrid the aggression is. She had to put some blood into it. Did she wish me dead or did she aim at marriage? All is compromise(d). Dioniris takes over and stirs the batter which follows his laws and gets all shrivelled up. Once cooked, it is no bigger than a fist. Where are the fine flours and the rising? There remains, distilled from a long story, this heterogeneous yet undetectable residue. The crêpe flops. It's a crêpe indeed. And its miracle: a whole much smaller and less appetizing than its parts. Anyway, there had never been any talk of marriage: one might as well believe China is smaller than the crêpe. No regret but one

out of a semifather's constraint and affliction for Dioniris has gone down beneath the wild floor

but I don't cry for what is loose cannot be loosened

except a sentence always the same a story of a single breath and without a pause and receive it henceforth [*d' ores*]★ as best you can out of desire or need and without taking it:

And since the flight seduces, seduction makes Dioniris' image rise and makes flee above my head the one who is not held back and who resembles no other between what is mortal and what is non-mortal

51

the one who is the lover of beautiful things what does he love?

Consider a human creature, a new protruding young man, giant, without being giant, through being wrenched from the ordinary space of a very big city, knowing it still but for having already reappeared later and been imposed to all creatures but you invisible consider a young man gay and present as one tears laughing at wrenching from a very big city its extraordinary power.

(For that, imagine a handwriting first slanting and ordinary on paper but this very handwriting then rising then washed then freed climbing multiplied, a handwriting of such force that it would no longer have to detach itself from the page but it would walk standing full letters ahead.) Consider a unique young real ordinary but singular man

let them become his!

young still in growth, but extraordinary, like two men in him alone, the one, unique, descended from memory and the other as unique and simultaneously on the descent poised at the angle of times where expectation fades ceaselessly. Handsome. Similar. Green to your most miserable most resigned most worked-up most losing desires. Handsome beyond what one could hope for. Red. It was impossible that he might exist, the one exactly who enveloping you would not restrict you and

yet would overrun you fortunately he was impossible
and it is the one who is exactly the one who looks like
no other. Beautiful and still more beautiful and the face
made crimson three times more beautiful than me

Himself enveloping himself fading and wrenching away
from himself surprising himself. He is walking outside
Pergamum between immense streets sunk deep
between higher walls, as if the city were upturned, the
walls pulled down, gliding at the tips of monuments: this
of course is just an effect, for he is now gliding on my
ordinary left and I am laughing my way down between
the walls of Pergamum: it's his way of walking that exor-
bitates buildings and reverses my point of view. Until
his way undoes itself and makes the walls of Pergamum
topple as if the gorge★ were upturned; without a foot
touching ground by dint of strength and lightness, walking so fast, so light, so dense that it is neither necessary
nor possible to touch the street with one's foot, thus
producing for my dilated eyes the very dance of desire
and and the corridor of his flight for which I adore him
I laugh I want nothing else until my death than this
willing than this corridor than this staggering dance and
these descending walls and till his death. And I never
stop not believing my faithfully dilated but struck eyes:
indeed this young, most powerful man still unknown
yesterday, destiny of today, is incredible to the eyes (but
he walks past and cuts out in the space of the very big
city the form of his movement)

Conceive of him on the model of the beloved rather than on the model of somebody who loves, without equal, desire him and pursue him as all-powerful and cunning in all things as the wild beloved.

Should He alone come near I shall have neither repose nor pause nor comma but I have touched named drawn him to me as does the lover with the beloved and the bird-catcher with the bird. Conceive of the young man, take the scissors, cut out, there he is, fixed smiling to himself unalterable and dead adored before any birth outside History and without chance, indifferent to the torment that you are, still ignorant of his own death, unknown, never seen, young and divinely blind at the exact point where the gods are who never look at death and thus do not know how to laugh. Look at him reach him hold him back. Forget to remember him, then forget oblivion if possible, irremediably once again and once again.

The desirable passes above my head and no sooner have I raised my hand to grasp him by his flame locks than an envious force throws itself across and

then from sea to sea one single big sea closing off the infinitely unfurled space of your plunged desire, gliding, shaking the cities where you wander in suspense, one single big chain of waters, the same ones, little by little; put the concatenation of waters between you and your fears and open your eyes and there in a shifting place which is neither somewhere on earth nor somewhere in the sky perhaps as in a dream the place

This is where, set down by the last link, indisputably elsewhere, I cannot fail to catch sight of a very young, very powerful, extraordinary man which would be nothing extraordinary if this man was named Adonis and if he popped out of the chest or if I was born more than once and elsewhere or if he was born ready-made in Persephony or if it was possible for a man to be another, in every single feature, which is impossible.

And if this impossible, no matter how impossible, is achieved, if you saw with your eyes by your living left side somebody who if he was dreamt would be in absolutely every single feature the one who you are not and whom you love and whom your desire prophesizes, and this being impossible, the young man who walks so fast in Pergamum is not impossible but real by chance, striking down, in every single feature but alive, the beloved whom one would have never seen

and no sooner have I raised my hand to grasp him than an envious force throws itself across and rage revolt and desire still lift me up

How to know how not to know how can the one be mine whom I covet barely born who in every single feature looks like the one whom Love tracks down?

Whom if he was mortal I would contend for with death. No sooner have I seen him alive than I lose land the ground eludes me and I elude the ground which is too hard too flat too elusive I lose time and that already I see his death.

If I opened the chest, I have not opened it yet, when I opened it, one would see the one who dying again is born again and whose fragrant breath holds death aloof from his desire. Open, fear, and breathe the unique smell of the one who can die twice

and fear lest you might not hold it back

If I lost it all that is real would wander from either edge of what is neither real nor nonreal.

Lovely mint allies me to all times, in all tenses.

Who of Dioniris or me sows the story who of the story or Him sows me who? If you see him pass above your head raise your hand, grasp him by the hair for the ungraspable may be yours.

We slept upstairs. At night, time flowed up our veins, the story avoided us. A red sheet covered us. I was pre-natal and old as the sea and He of an ancient age which nothing can blemish and which can pass off as child-hood. I adored him I touched him no sooner had I touched him than I thought of his death. Time here did not follow time, angled death or death angle. He was going up and it was no time it was joy, it was a blood, an emulsion of memory and death, going up in one and the other body and overflowing the state of life the state of present the state of reality.

He: Orphan, son of his death, and I impossible prophetic memory: for in a near future he would be dead so was I taught by his moist lips and he had turned his tongue seven times in my mouth. What his mouth knows my mouth knows He put his death in my mouth. I sucked it and chewed it. It had been understood that he would be dead.

What age was Dioniris for me the same age aloof from time as Adonis for his death. He had said: 'Remember yourself.' And thinking of the way in which the dead think themselves and of what they think of being dead he had said: 'Remember us.' One should now always rethink the number of love. It would all pass through more than two and not far from three and by chance or ill chance it would all pass through three plus or minus one and one of us three should be the dead one. But it is impossible to know which one of us is less dead, and through what also Three passes, or pass, or does not pass, but, an angled figure, unites and supports times. He summoned me to remembrance, I became body or text or active tomb and nothing was but what would already have been, and all was but fated to return. Hearing him I heard myself in advance hearing him again, and I was more than one.

she walking on his right no longer knowing whether I had already wanted and expected him, if I was in front or someone else was, if I had come from before or if I was descended from after, if I adored him because he was dead or if he was going to die because I adored him. I was descending between the walls of Pergamum, my body burnt with a mortal joy, the geometrical place of chances, at the blind angle of revelations: I saw him with the eyes that would have seen him dead and seeing my eyes as they would see then. Thus, leaning from either edge, but without toppling and touching sea or land with either foot, and I between two dead but without touching the death of either body, we descend between the foreign walls of Pergamum, and leaning light and surviving we reach the Garden of Disappearances where all that flees is desirable.

I, believing I am dreaming, believing I dreamt without any remarkable difference between the dreaming state and the waking state. Impossible to know whether my eye was besetting the dream's sides in order to skirt round them or whether it ascended the sides itself in order to believe it was dreaming, breaking loose from the soft embrace of Love's arms, it runs away between clouds and lights and leaves me: see the shining star flee from the sky and shoot in the night away from the eye which adores it, see Adonis starving his Love. Playing life against death to the naked eye. And finally a difference, I, the eye risked to the limits, forced to think the unthinkable to see the bones through the body, drunk from no longer being able to avoid his death in my eye in reality and his corpse across my desire, and craving to the very extremities with all my strengths to remain risked on either edge, to live by death by the eyes the veins the sex the thought, now a pulverized body now a furious scratched crumpled narrative, a nerveless leaf; and dreading losing sight of her one moment and then dying from it.

To sleep no more: thus did my hearthless dreams irrupt, terrible and final, into Peruvia and unto this day and they made their disappearances in broad daylight. I was tottering between listening and silence, tensed to breaking point and stuck at an angle with myself I was fluttering about broken above my life's corridor, driven away from either edge, and all my feelings were inordinate: for he was not dead yet and we knew he was already dead and that was his almighty power. I never had a rest. He was walking without setting foot. I never asked myself questions. Without a break, life in overbid. Now the left side went lower, now the right side went lower and I saw in it a sign of general anxiety. What he said here was heard there. I could see myself seeing the giant monuments bend and wobble through all those troubled eyes that come to me from death. And I was looking at him, then I thought I was losing him, then I was looking at him. He could have disappeared at every moment he was apparent he was no longer quite there I was watching him now I remembered now later and that later I would cry and I will have cried, I was crying but I was holding back my tears, but I was already spilt, he was a young man, incredibly mortal and powerful, who made one die and rise again. There were extraordinary squirrels among the trees of Disappearance: big fast mute squirrels hurling themselves from top to bottom with the motionlessness of stones. They could be seen flying about in all directions but always from top to bottom, diving so abruptly that they caused space to spurt. I thus cast my eyes into time so fast and violently that I give the deadline a jolt. There were bitter dangerous plants and climbing evergreens.

In the end we would be caught up. I am expected in the future by scissors, but the hands that holds them is trembling, and I'm trying hard to hold it back and I cannot manage to see it. The scissors look like they're opening by themselves and from all eternity. The squirrels tumble by themselves like detached stones or ripe fruit by chance or recurrence. They land on a strange meadow which is not a meadow but one of those speaking things which hail me wherever I go again: a meadow or a field, in any case a book, organic, vegetative, open, its pages written with ivy. Here I am subjected to the ivy test. Everyone knows that ivy is a sign of marriage and that the sign of marriage is a sign of marriage with death.

Read the strange book of Disappearances: the left page, big as a very big bed, is less cramped than the right page which has the appearance of a dense surface, without spaces [?], unpleasant to the eye which is struck by a strange reddish glow from the leaves. *He* does not read the ivy-text but wants me to read it aloud. I understand nothing from it. The agitated leaves scatter their meaning and sometimes are even pulled down and I can see their dull other side. Others cleverer than me could read in my place: fearless, futureless, deathless women, sometimes pregnant, without difficulties. It seems that I am the only one who cannot. I jib, I declare that I cannot read because this text is a fake text, because it is illegible: its dense surface of mobile leaves is but an inextricable metaphor and the word illegible itself, all cramped within its own letters, is illegible.

This book has nothing to read: it grows and covers up. This is what I say first in a calm voice then in an increasingly hurried voice and one more and more high-pitched then by shouting so as to make myself heard by what we will be later and I throw myself onto the left page from which I rip out handfuls of rustling crackling bitter leaves while shedding angry tears, with full bare hands with revolt and defiance that's what my soul is. The squirrels flee into the tangle of ivy and become wild letters. I will not have read what grows and covers up I rip off pages and strip bare and I set about digging once more weeping for Dioniris the source of sap has run dry.

I hold him by the waist, my arm thrust round his waist is throbbing too, his body is the cross between the forces of life and the work of death, and the body of confrontation. We walk. We leap across the ivy field, where we go in truth we go again. What I have said will be better understood later, I am speaking in the time when he no longer hears: I don't know what I think, I will know it when I no longer think. I am thrown against the flow of the present: that time is all built like a tomb waiting for me, prior chest of my death. Its huge shadow makes a semblance of present for me and conceals the present from me. There's the present. In the present a door appears. I open. The present opens. I rush in. I fall. There's the present.

The lover and the beloved are the two vases of the sand-glass. The sands flow from one into the other. Love turns the sand-glass upside down. Desire flows from one into the other the beloved exhausts the lover then the lover overturns the beloved in order to love him then the beloved takes back from the lover the product of love in order to exhaust it then the lover overturns love in order to be loved then the beloved overturns love inexhaustibly and there's no present. Desire falls from one to the other body

I can reach Dioniris if he can be reached behind the wall of the Garden where the future is the past of the present on the reverse of all where desire sets the other desire in motion where life does without a body

and the sun does without time where what is nowhere
beneath the watery floor, is

repeating the course of pain at the memory of pain
and return of the memory of pain which begets
another pain which returns to my heart and so on,
between the motionless linings of my throat, striking
and producing where he strikes the wall to be struck
with my wailings. I am speaking to him now from this
constricted tender and fluvial throat which is already
reeling, scratched, broken with an inaudible readiness
to let itself be heard from the waking state to the
dreaming state. A song of blood rises which I will spill
later when I am still alive.

You are the first dead, the first to die.
Move, move, we are being expected,
What does he think where he is when he thinks forward, among his fathers where is he when the front
catches up with the rear.

And now silence here; him among the silence
What does he think where he is

*Move move for time is what is neither present nor
non-present until where yester eve* [l'hier]★ *divides into here
and desire divides into desires and each desire is desire desiring
itself more and more*

I see a motionless squirrel does he see it? Actually I don't see a squirrel, I see only a semibody amid the illegible page. The leaves had concealed it, but now that I've ripped them off I see it, unavoidable. The thing, being, this motionless thing is buried is motionless is small as half a squirrel but immense, a stunning infinity like the history of death. Does Dioniris have eyes to see this thing cut down the middle, buried already but not quite, plunged head first in the frozen bed of all things, either by luck or actually by decision: the beast would have dug its own death nest, would have burrowed into it, sunk into it, but not quite, would be dead before burying itself, would have hidden its own death from itself before dying, would have neglected out of indifference the lower sublunar part of the body, would have provided only for the extinction of its eyes, would have thrown itself from a tree with such death strength that it would have sunk belly-deep into the loose earth, would bequeath to air and sun its hair and decomposition, would have stifled its anguished cries in the earth: or else the squirrel, driven by some urge unknown to us, has madly thrown itself into some unknown hole and trapped itself to death there. In the attitude of desire, of excavation, of constraint, sunk belly-deep, stiff as a stone. If I had not seen it, I might have tripped over this thing. However small it might be and far I cannot but see it: its marvellous motionlessness makes me discover how much the universe, even in its arrested, mineral, heavy and recumbent parts, is vibrant, is the finest, most persistent movement. I am thinking: You're the first dead, the first to die. Move, move and catch up with my fathers.

Neither above ground nor below ground but in between or half dead the motionless semibody, a cut of which being?

What can die there before my eyes dying three steps away from my trembling memory? What makes my tongue turn and my fury rise? and my desire turn topsy-turvy. If abruptly possessed with a new rage I jumped on him with my feet together, if I heeled it in level with the ground. If I touched with my foot this stiffened bit wrapped in soft grey hair in order to feel the soft-and-hard? What if I finished off this corpse too much of a corpse

The things one mustn't do, shouldn't one do them? (And if once more split in two we walked in the Garden of Disappearances similar to those characters whose bas-relief profile can be seen on walls sawed in two down the middle of our nose, in the fashion of those whom the gods sever more than once . . .)

Backtracking, attracted, me by the thing, him all throbbing by me, we are now carried away by the irresistible towards the point of sinking. I will see, I will touch, I will desire, I will crush. Perhaps I will tremble with horror. Does he see what my eyes see? Then he would see these big scissors. I would rush to get ahead of him. These are my cutting scissors. I would catch the squirrel by the tail, I would cut him down the middle as one severs a branch. Something in the way the blades of the scissors are crossed gives me a peculiar satisfaction. The effect of a knife or of an axe would be altogether different: I want that to open and to close. Then I put down the piece of squirrel remaining in my hand directly above the earth. With each step that brings us nearer the burrowing hole I am nagged again by the idea that the very same thing happened to a person that was dear to me or who is very near and dear to me and so near that I can feel their convulsive starts through my own limbs. I would tell him or her (this person) this: 'I read the description of a particularly awful trick performed in the East: One slices up a living squirrel, etc.' I would then notice a complex and weird expression on their face, an expression which I could not describe otherwise than as being the horror of an intense pleasure unknown to the very person, yet I would not hesitate to tell it to them, should it cost me an arm and a leg for nothing I don't know why could compel me to silence and the same horror the same intense pleasure the same ignorance would run through me simultaneously at the idea that it would be happening to a person dearer to me than my own life and my face would be marked by a strange and horribly tormented, yet impersonal expression, the executor being neither me nor him nor anybody anyway for the cutting was being carried out impersonally: before my eyes. So that, heading without resistance towards the point of sinking it is impossible to know whether I am trembling with fright or whether I am trembling because he, so near and dearer to my eyes than my own life, transmits to my limbs the throbbings of his mortal desire carried backwards by an obscure and impersonal force, or whether I am trembling from desire and from desiring what I must desire, should it cost me an arm and a leg, which, if I kept it secret from him, through an inordinate effort compelling me to impossible silence, in the same stroke would flood my reason, which if I tell it to him floods my reason, which if it came true, without however my being the executor, but came true, would deprive me of the person who is dearer to me than my own life, or whether I am trembling from the fright of the desire which desires me to death, which if it did not come true would fell me, would split me asunder in the eyes of the very near and dear person walking right now beside me without setting foot on any of the known lands, whose limbs are swollen with my own blood and whose bones my life contends for with his death, whose eyes, if they closed, would throw my eyes to the waters' restless night, which now open before my eyes do not see what I believe I see and which tears my lids with the nails of destiny. I want to see that, at the cross of the known lands and of the unknowable colours of the sky, where the Bed opens which will keep our smell when we have ceased making love for centuries.

And if in a bad sleep you sheared the only man who ever resembled the adored one in every single feature, and if your eyes which believed they were opening fell into the blood issuing from this body so dear, shed by yourself, wouldn't you have been thrown to the ground among the dead? And if on a bad path, borne by counterfeiting chance, you tripped over the corpse wrapped in grey hair of a nameless beast, wouldn't you be struck by the idea that this thing has not been put there by chance,

I saw everything, I did not know if He could see everything, I knew that the buried squirrel, because it was buried, cut us to pieces, I did not hold back my eyes which were falling, with the horrible gravity of stone eyes, and nothing held back my thoughts. No sooner had we taken three steps running than I had known and cried more than once ten thousand deaths and I had killed, buried and unearthed it more than ten thousand times and the whole earth with all its states

Was riddled with our squirrels' bodies. A thousand pillar arms could not have supported this bowl of deaths. I threw myself into it in my mind, thought myself as dust, wishing to cover our pieces by myself, and if I had been ten thousand widows I would not have found enough tears, for one only

There was in the Garden of Disappearances a fat grey half-buried squirrel which was reminiscent of the death of the Only One. It was impossible for me to have seen it without my thoughts splitting asunder and my suddenly withered life losing itself on the unlimited edge of its death. Big scissors were watching and cutting nascent thoughts down the middle.

And each half missing its own half mated with it and they intertwined in their desire to merge into a single being, in a time made up of the time that remains and of the time that does not remain.

There are still three steps remaining. I will squat down, I will observe him, I will see his hair quiver in the wind, I will open my hand, I will put forward my hand which I will no longer look at, open celestial unknown to myself appearing with hollow palm splayed fingers, and I will let it touch the semibody, barely, barely, he will be dead and the hand will be alive. I had never touched a dead being with my fingers. I will have already forgotten the softness of the touch, I caressed my fingers on Him yester eve or the day before yester eve. The softness of my hand is now matched only by the softness of anguish. Life withdraws its waters from my body, hope leaves my body, a strange weakness suffuses and takes me. Does he move away from his centre down the dreaded ways does he neglect himself? Pieces of squirrels covered with foliage kiss my sight of himself when he is not next to me and I'm the one who piled them up. I hide so as not to see him

perish now. A time says: 'And now today he is still alive.'
And now? And it will exclaim: 'And now today he is
decomposed' or 'And there he was still alive then' and
I think that I will think he was alive, I think he is alive,
and we are living then, and if I write he will be dead
and if I don't write he will die and I will read the book
of yester eve. If I ripped off the leaves if I tore the legible which is too legible if I decomposed them, before
. . . all that will have never taken place.

So what would be forgotten by whom?

Isn't the most legible the most dangerous? Can
oblivion forget oblivion? How to untie what is not
already tied, what is dying is alive

once again you ivy do lament and once more for I
am coming to wrench your harsh heads apart for
Dioniris died his death and the remorseless earth has
closed back on his precious head

in full life it crosses my mind that He is there, two
or three steps away from us, buried waist-deep, long
dead and as foreseen and I see him dead, as it would be
written but there's still time not to see and for disappearance to divide and in dividing to disappear

There's still time to wrench him away from the
hole, if I saved him, he would live, how come I did not

think about it first, I rush, I've already lost age-old minutes, I saw him dead beforehand before he disappeared, but if I manage to save him you will not take the road of my fathers either.

Yourself through Yourself with Yourself

Thus before my eyes: the squirrel, the split earth, death, split time, and war: the squirrel against burial, the earth against death, my desire against time, the desire of time against Him, against us, against the semibodies

Life sinks before my eyes . . . and I barely raise my hand in order to grasp it by its tuft,

He desires, the one who produces desire: What does he desire?

The squirrel was waiting for us, waiting for our bodies bound by trembling. It must have been waiting for us for ten thousand years perhaps in order to send us back dead to death, it having being dead from time immemorial, therefore never dead, therefore always, actually: unavoidable.

Haven't I crossed the seas poured end to end, haven't I travelled through the lands which separate the East from the West and the seas that separate the West from the East haven't I opened my memory to

Persephony and Persephony to memory. I haven't learnt the most diverse and the most modern languages, I haven't been forgotten a thousand times by a thousand provisional hunted semifathers and haven't I a thousand times fled from a thousand successive sourmothers, I haven't fled, haven't stumbled, snapped, wavered, waited, despaired, enough to make several women's lives or several men's lives of my times

I haven't escaped from the Symplegades. I haven't travelled past the land of the Amazons; and that of the Chalybes who do not cultivate the earth, do not breed livestock and live entirely off the benefits from their smithies; and the land of Tibareni, where husbands are in the habit of moaning as if they were in labour when their wives are about to give birth; and the land of Mossynoeci who live in wooden castles, all mate together and bear disproportionately long lances and white ivy-leaf-shaped shields in order to manage to lose by chance or recurrence at the inconceivable angle of times the unexpected one who for me makes the past be present and the future more than imperfect, with every single feature, definitive and still never known beforehand and henceforth the unavoidable face of the one I would have loved if he had waited for me; and haven't I missed the only one—very near, very dear, the dearest in the eyes of my memory, at the moment when I discover him, haven't I put into play reason, law, cause, order, books, cities with unshakeable buildings, Peruvia till expiry in order to trip over the visible part of a big grey squirrel indifferent to continuity, to the influence of stars, to us?

To desire

The order has been given. And the smell of Lovely Mint wafts up, recognizable above all others. Out of terror and loneliness I fell to the ground. My body in an arc. And now, Desire,
    Believe the unbelievable
    Believe death to be dead
    Believe the last dead to be the last
    Believe you see the image reflect its prey to the
    light
    Unsay what is said
    Throw yourself to the ground: it will flow
    Make your self-confidence out of the uncertain
    Put disappearance next to appearance like the lover
    next to
    love
    And take my eyes to see him
    Jump
    Wrenched the head with dazzled eyes from the
    lascivious earth
    Fleeing
    Exactly in the terrified, distraught way of a
    squirrel caught between two leaps
    Take the history of Nations, undo the age-old
    tissue the courses and causes and give each time

back to itself and you will be ravished by the
great Movement

I remembered I had the time to touch it, barely,
with my fingertips. From close up, his hair was less grey,
whiter, more ginger-coloured, very long and fairly stiff
to the fingers. It looked like a big furry rat to me. Its
mouth was full of earth and other things. The leaves
trembling from the leap that carried it away were
crumpling a kind of stammering discourse.

*No sooner do I raise my hand to grab it than another
force comes athwart and loss defiance desire here's my soul*

She on its left as Time on the left of Eternity: uncertain, distraught, adoring uncertainty, returned to my
sender so that he sends me back, not knowing any more
whether I adore him because he is not dead or whether
he is not dead so that I adore him for uncertainty.
Indecisive.

*Can the illegible be legible? If you want to read,
jump, do not set yourself so much as a comma*

It is Dioniris who frightened him, Him laughing,
supposedly alive. I'd no longer looked at him for three
minutes, or perhaps two or four, yet I'd seen him dead,
alive, dying, cut, dead, severable, lost, buried, dead, seen.
Or this squirrel. Suspended above us walking without

setting foot among the leaves but leaping across these illegible pages, death makes its headline after the event. This is why I couldn't but leaf through the ivy-text lying there without head or tail,—but for having seen the squirrel's tail—, dense, agitated in all directions by the abrupt flight of the whole animal which, this very moment, had seemed to me without head. It wrenches itself away from earth! Escaped comma

Before my eyes now the ivy bed, uninterrupted. I think of the invisible roots which go down, dig, burrow, mingle and knot suck pump and get clogged up illegible. And the roots lead me into the mantle of the earth and so on by sinking and clearing a path, plunging eyeless directionless towards the big red burning belly which dilates and contracts and dissolves me. I, patient among the maternal, nuptial strata. I could carve out a tomb for him among the strata. The blood gets cold among the veins. A wooden tomb full of herbs and spices and I would keep him far from daylight.

It would be a bed without edges, cradled by the earth itself, moving. This bed wanders [*lit erre*]★ . . .

I fear to shout the Intervention of the story and the bitter taste of the nether plants the lid which is pulled down and the rocks which get nearer. I fear the recumbent knife which slits love down the middle, the law of genders which separates the one from the other and the other from its identical self and which summons you here and summons me there, I fear the gap and the order of bodies and the invidious Fury. And the Intervention says: Thou shalt not lie in the same tomb.

But there will be this open bed among the veins, barely breathing, and, in the red glow of the earth, marvellously white, which will look at nobody, which will look only at us, keeping us. Losing us as well with the help of time, to the point of effacement. It is this forbidden bed where we will undo each other and ourselves which will break up the earth and mark the story.

The location of the bed was all designated among the ivies in the splinter of earth incised by the squirrel. I saw us there. We would go to Peruvia on this honeymoon. It would be an incessant, immutable trip: Peruvia would take care of the change of setting by itself, would produce now its mountains, now its overturned depths, now its troubled seas, now its deserted floors, on the limitless edges of our bed, it would deploy in front of our amused eyes the treasures of its gifts, the hidden story of its life, the visible story of its life and the unknown story of its sex well before our appearance, and we, acting on the unconceived, pre-genetic, perhaps absent edges except for being the very movement which Peruvia commands through our eyes, or for the future chance of its indifferent sex or for making Peruvia's sex play, incised and why not a body of incision, or better still we, an unmarked sex knowing from time immemorial that the loser takes all at the game of life, not fearing to omit in the bed where we are actively lost any distinctive feature, master of chief illusions, as inseparable as the honeymoon from Peruvia, as our rapture from our motionless bones, (it would have been necessary, in order to separate us, to bring about one more genesis and yet another one)

As my desire from the Garden of Disappearances, as Pergamum from our stubbornness, as the squirrel from the adored young man, as my terror from my adoration and from my rage, and as our story from its Parchment

I was of loneliness daughter of my terror, fallen to the ground. I had then stopped checking the most precious features for three bad minutes. Or else he felt the waves of my fall,—for thus buried he did not hear or see at least doubtless he could perceive the minutest unrest of the earth—, or Dioniris having suddenly aimed at the buried semibody a small stone actually clipped him, whatever the case may be the intact animal wrenched itself away from the entrails with such vigour that I gave a start. He, the Most Near, laughed long at my sudden jolt. I watched him laughing. I took this laughter with my lips, with my teeth, I sucked it, ate it, drugged myself with it, vowed it to eternity, heard it after centuries, for the walls of time would send it back

to me out of commiseration. I can still hear him leaving
at the time when I hear him rising above my head and
not returning, perhaps he will return later by chance
and out of stubbornness from either edge.

No sooner had I lost sight of him for three minutes
than I shuddered with terror: What if he had wasted
away though? What if he had changed? What if during
my wandering on the limitless edges of the text, fascinated as I was and hoodwinked by the squirrel and the
commaless time, he had already moved away from himself? He was laughing, supposedly alive. Laughter was
pulling his lips and eyelids tight, baring his teeth, veiling
his eyes it was still him, but less near, his most slender
body tensed, shaken, I was sure that this laughter tore
the most fragile tissues and I did not take my eyes off
it, my eyes held it tight, watching out for imperceptible
jolts. It seemed to me that I had not seen him for a
thousand years. I cast ten thousand glances plus one at
him: these ten thousand glances turned round this
known but never known-enough body and made a
shining ring for it, less shining than the sole sheer pen-
etrating look which I let fall on his very being, dashing
straight between his laughter and his death till the
lighted depths of his life, there where he was exactly at
the centre of his story, a centre lost at once even though
I did have the time to stare deep into it, this longest
day of his story, similar to the stare Eratosthenes of
Alexandria shed into the dried-up bottom of the well

at Syene, on the edge of the Nile. For this stare Eratosthenes had travelled five thousand stadia under an exhausting sun. And I had to wait five thousand years in order to live the ephemeral instant when the bottom surfaced, when Peruvia split open Persephony's convulsive bark when the rays of sense rose in suspension at a sheer angle with this story in a straight line so precise that any trace of shadow was ruled out, he was Alone, bedless, unadulterated, without circumstance, unrivalled or without comparison.

Himself through Himself with Himself, visible simple being eternal and incorruptible.

Everything I am saying from and till here will be what will have always been inexact and approximate at most without ever being able to approximate the Most Near as near as possible. What I mean is that at this moment one could have said that he was his bare name, but that would be inexact unfortunately.

And Only the One always present

On the one hand I rejoiced over the squirrel's disappearance. On the other hand its disappearance disturbed me: it prompted me with the fear that he might owe his life only to disappearance. Will I have to lose him in order to keep him? Or, keeping him, will I have to lose him? Again those questions which would take

my whole life and more if I so much as attempted to
pose them but which would leave me no respite if I
dismissed them. They draw their lives from the very
heart of my life. Persist,

>   return
>
>   return
>
>   return

and by dint of decomposing me
compose me
and this has been going on for three or six years
  ;   goes after me   a thousand years   and another
    thousand
and surely, drive me further and further

>   nearer and nearer my
>
>   incompletion

and by dint of digging
make bed for me
but without a river

>   and push me and lay me down

but without a river
and thrown from either edge
of the riverless bed I swim between a thousand terrifying rocks in the long run I trace with my body
the figures of this questioning
I take some pleasure and some breath from it
I am taken by sorrow
and this pleasure this breath this sorrow
regulate the cruel step of lovers

It is most obvious that we are dealing here with a reciprocal work: I am worn out but I wear out. I fall and I set upright. I am lying but I rise. I lay down and am raised. I see and I am seen. The ballet of the cruel is cruel and almost unbearable to imagine: the dancers chosen for their beauty and their youth whirl about and chase one another on a narrow stage with high walls. They give themselves over to the order of the rhythm, they are doomed to perdition. Each sees the other without seeing himself, and each absent to himself is detained by the other's mystery, without knowing he has a body apt to capture that one, thus each fleshed by each other and himself fleshless, thrown towards the uncapturable, figures the hopeless step of disjunction, each produces his own perdition and his shimmering, a blind dancer of the ballet of deposition, where the sun eclipses itself into its shadow, rigorously. Thus the dance plays the dancers, thus the scissors play the body of love, blinding plays the dance of blinding, thus what cannot be found finds its rigour and its disappointment. And each beautiful being suspends his being on the verge of the eyes of each youthful being, in the expectation of seeing himself, and the desire produces Adonis' chest

At one moment or the other the dancers collapse out of breath and often die in the dance, they're here, there, farther away, self-ignored but cruelly visible, lying recumbent on the limitless edges of the dance, as if they had never danced or desired, or pursued, or lived and as if only they had dreamt or the dance had secreted them then dropped them there, farther and nearer just as the sea marks out its retreat. The dance on its verge happening outside the dancers, lying recumbent, inverted, deposed sovereigns, at either time. In the meantime the blind, handsome, young, whirling, firmly wove the single gold linen without knowing how. Perhaps, lying down, they dream of seeing themselves dancing, but we cannot know it, in this moment. The dream or death received them. We in the trembling present do not know what they know. Who can I be, blurred as I am by what I am going to cease being, the blind production of a future which holds my eyes in anticipation of its power and keeps the present blood hostage so as to release it when we don't know what to do with it, who am I, I who am led to go through future ages in order to come back down on a ground already shivering from the announced rifts. The time will come when we could know what we are now unaware we know, when the invisible will give way to the visible; when the ivy-text will speak, and I can see the shadow of this time gathering above us, but when the visible has overtaken the invisible who can tell whether the visible will not allow the invisible to be seen, and that we will have eyes to lose in it?

The earth around us damp rolled up in the gold linen

Tacit, under the squirrel's sign, without however this man So Close having said to me he had noticed it, we were living beforehand and by return, so that I could hear us talking through our teeth and where fear catches hope by the throat, sometimes hope feigned certainty, simultaneously through lost and withheld discourse, in the decomposed present, most often in a very loud voice hastened by the imminence of aphonia. There escaped questions from me which made me feel uneasy, for no sooner had I spoken three words than the sentence leaked sense in the way a burst hull would leak water. They were wild questions which sought a target and eluded it, and which persisted then returned, returned, returned to the point of wondering about themselves as return and this insistence began to look like a dance but on the spot, and which did not need an answer. They made a story whose outside was time and each sentence made a provisional world.

'You yourself Dioniris . . .'

No sooner had I shot an arrow than too late I wished I hadn't but too late. The voice of storm has no louder ring, the time all around us was nothing more than the echoing stone which reflects the radiant splendour of Him.

Seek the surest sentence for me, Love, give me the most searing tongue give me the scathing shaft with which I will strike home and reach him without losing him!

Ten times I rushed on the trail of the shaft, but no sooner had I uttered three words, 'You yourself later Dioniris did you . . .' but no sooner had I uttered three words than my lips tore apart the sentence cut my tongue my voice fell and I lost burning tears yet O Love I must say it, I will not rest until I have reached him! with an unforgiving sentence, a surest, least hesitant sentence! Until I hit him without wounding him. And losing my tears, my courage and my breath but not the strength of my desire I returned to it 'Later Dioniris you yourself . . .

I twisted the shaft and I shot it with the patient fury of the bird-catcher in love with the bird, I challenged him and I strained my voice and my breath furiously and once more then with another breath fainter but subtler than the halting breath I resumed:

'Yourself then later you,

but no sooner has *you* grazed *later* than my throat bursts open and the sentence sags, carrying away my hopes and my desire in its collapse, and yet I desired its resumption ever more rigorously and cruelly, then already walking alongside silence, but still on this side of silence with my tongue almost dead, I ventured to set time on fire again and said: 'Did you later' but no sooner had *later* touched *you* than the sentence broke and collapsed, then the waters of sense flowed into the unspeakable and lost themselves in it, my question wandered from one place to the other of the non-known, *late* pushed *you* back, and *you* wounded *later*, but my

desire was the place of their impossible climax and my
heart was the place of my desire, and the secret place
of my heart was produced by the impossible climax,
and I was myself the place of the secret place, suspended
to the encounter of the most dear and the future.

My unique and most powerful desire is the one
which enjoys my immortality

Near the iridescent female immortality which
brings to the world an offspring in its liking and in mine

lies my desire, immortal and male, and which
enjoys it.

Another one leaves it, having finished enjoying it
passionately similar to its desire which I desire.

What was cut by the question whereby the question was cut was the bed of our immortality.

The sweet moment when we will no longer speak
cannot be delayed much longer.

If my tongue was my desire it would have known
our immortality. Now my tongue was dying, at the
tomb of my mouth, and I could not risk it any longer.

Such as off the shores of Disknowledge but in sight
of its edges the fissured craft loads up, sinks and settles
at the immersed roots of Disknowledge.

Such as off death's shores the question sank without any word. What desire dug, fate invaded. A tongue less torn than mine would have launched its own story. But mine was tearing.

Through another mouth could perhaps have been said: 'Will you later like to be the comma which orders the text?' And through another: 'Will you Dioniris Yourself later be yourself with yourself still and with me?'

My voice: sacrificial, red, knowledgeable, ignorant, rings loud and covers the incapable face of its inaudible; the one, before the throat, which bathes amid tears. There was a text from the heart which kept inscribing its silence without breaking it without rest without comma without life therefore without breath therefore without danger unshakeable in sentences poignant no ear no body other than mine orphaned to be which was not written by writing which was not heard by hearing through which writing was written without signs it was a never-heard never-learnt litany written while trembling bearing the complaint from one to the other blank which like non-death I held dearer than life for the simple reason that it inscribed itself in the present without a break by carrying without taking the story into account the present in preternal mood which gives short shrift to memory and a certain unknown regular

irregular chained broken incorrigible distance from my
lips from my heart from my veins from my fingers:

'Unforgettable no sooner have I warned my eyes of
your face
'It seems to my eyes that they didn't see you
'For a thousand years, Three times more beautiful than
me
'For a thousand years
'Who am I, I who lose centuries in three looks and you
'Who are you, for whom memory bursts open
'The monstrous chests of time and I
'Who abandons me?
'Haven't I planted superb gardens for you
'Haven't I adored your doors
Haven't I composed my face for you
Nothing beautiful which I have omitted doing towards
you
I have put my left side at your service and my right side
serves you
I have spoken to you when you were not listening
Unforgettable the unforgettable holds me
And now who to address this complaint to?

We were walking back up between two edges of eternity at the exit of the Garden of Disappearances now calm now enraged, lively, alarmed, furtive, trying to pick a quarrel with the decrees of Fate, sparkling with the amorous challenge, anxiety was following us, swimming between the monumental walls of the Street of Walls, burning, frail, dashing towards the exhausting probable, deprived of chance: all the gold at stake in the businesses the world conducts and all the gold the world eats and the gold crust of the earth and beneath the crust the upper gold mantle and the gold of the lower mantle and the gold roots of continents, if it was melted down again, would not buy us another story, not even a hesitation of our story, and yet we would not have yielded one of the sparkling seconds through which, chained up, we were so strongly so poorly armed, rather high death than the lower part of chance, ourselves, suffused with the invisible gold of ourselves, very precious and rare and losing out richly, almost not playing any longer soon won't be playing, forlorn,

But still alive here absolutely covered with prophetic eyes.

But immediately still we happily silent or perhaps silently happy reflect back to the sun its vain light, more sparkling between the armed walls than a gold river, of a youth so clear that it allows traces of youth to be seen at all points, a young gold which does not allow itself to be seen; deprived between shores but fabulously rich in signs which our gazes released. Nobody had seen what the world allows to be seen when it is seen except us all eyes, and our eyes all body and our bodies all fire and honey, and of honey and fire our sexes, making our bed from the world and from our bed the big folded page of our knowledge: we were rolling in it with laughter, with beauty, with fear, with desire, the one on and in the other in and on the one and on the book without being mindful of syntax, I sentence in flight, even without a subject, short of designating any word as head, laying myself open to commas, provoking them even, he diving onto my body, agitated, striking, over- turning, interrupting, forcing me to move back, to con- tradict myself, in one single breath, but gaily. Without him I would have been dumb. We were composing in vague leaps and retreats and wild outbursts an unfath- omable text which, had it had a reader or a god to aim at, would have disturbed the order of effects and senses and driven the eye away, but we whom it exposed would not have the time to read it and I often forgot to think about it, sinking, itself inking shadows of silences which I could not hear without shivering, in the folds of the white seas,

I don't weep I don't weep, for the one who makes me grieve is still alive,

However he may have descended beneath the pages of waters later

perhaps I will weep

If I have not wept yet it is because I still have not found in the hollow of a land the grave where I will be able to lay him down calmly in a gold sheet and cover him with ivy

He the pages I the sails he the breath I the fright he the skiff I the frightful crumpling of sails he the risk I the swirl and memory he the oblivion I the sentence fixed by the comma, I the blind face notched but by him, I the vague billow unfurled he running on the sea without getting wet *deus, deus ille, Adonaïs,* unruffled

I will weep later

I

Will be the wreck of our story, five fathoms of memory deep lay my calmed body and his body recumbent on the ocean bed

And here farther: his head, like a simple star, with a red face, detached,

Who can boast having seen in reality the head of the god he has dreamt of?

Conceive of the divine head. Conceive of a defenceless bodiless head adrift rolled along the watery floor in the wake of the unsailed vessel. Seen from above this detached young Orphic head arouses my attention, my pity, my desire too, most acute, to have known its body. I look at it through the wet hair through the wings of the nose through the parted lips which breath once shunned: floating but still washed away carrying knotted in its hair the long currents of waves inventing an effect of flight through the lost breathing through the suspension of a smile through the arched strength of the eyebrows and sunken cheeks. It was flying high when it fell, I thought, and I wish I had known its body. Man or woman, who cares, it was a peerless being and I could have loved it. These lips once spoke, they freeze into a twitch at the corner, if only I had heard him I would have known the truth, which truth, that which is the simplest, the most for-midable, my search, the one absolute which is not an answer and is not a question, which is what flees from me and, as it flees from me, eludes me, as does the figure of my figure, beautiful and urging me to the chase. I would give all the water of the world to have known him as a body. It has known. It still knows in silence what I cannot know. My eyes on these lips on these eyelids find this mystery beautiful and terrible. It seems that if Love was Death it would have looked like him if he was dead or Adonis. Desire freezes me into beholding this absolute head which carries the seas away in its hair. Each feature of this face invokes a continuation and yet each feature is self-sufficient, the contingency of limbs, the exaltation of eyes forehead and nose, the necessity of a sex, the placeless beloved drifts away, an absolute head without the obligation of a body but where each feature inscribes the waters without an obligation of sense or direction, where each line is a sex. Reigning supreme over the surface, with liquidated body, its bed is everywhere

Hold out your arm, to grab it by its locks if you can

(And I too wanted to make our bed everywhere with lost edges where the land can be the sea and close its sheets of waters on us and where men sleep with gods)

I hold out my arm I want to grab the divine head by its bitter hair for it is exactly the head I dreamt of and I want to drag it by the hair into reality.

I did not grab it I did not drag it I did not hold its wet hair and I still dream it exactly divine

Or else compare my story to a statue with well-regulated proportions, representing a human creature larger than life, draped in some dress with generous folds and fairly far away from the body, with a head full of impossibly tangled locks a big nose a closed mouth the pose of the whole equivocally nonchalant, the head in truth elsewhere, twisted round with a movement of the neck outside the folds, such that the space around would be marked by some fictitious momentum: one would notice that the statue simulates an impossible movement except in a dream, it would walk backwards in time, its back turned away from the decrees of stars but its magnetized head irresistibly tempted by reality, and if one could turn it, to see where it is looking, what one would discover would not lack violence—this head is eyeless but the eyes are not lost or vain—they are fixed up there among the stars at an incalculable distance from their orbits, and polar, and the head points blindly in the direction of what is lost: if Alpha of Cepheus made the Earth move instead of letting it come into its axis, and if the earth moved five or six thousand years in anticipation, disturbing the order of time, seasons, attractions, it would oscillate the way the statue oscillates under the spell of its foreseeing eye.

Often I muse about the dream, about the statue, about what is known, I close my eyes and I see myself.

Often when I look with my insufficiency at this young man, unhoped for promised and forbidden greater in his smallness than the greatness of the universe

I see that my story turns me by recurrence, that I am in the shadow of what is in store for me, shaken to the bones by what I will be when the future has caught up with me in the present, that moving forward I am deposed and that I am knowable from the point of view of the unknowable only, and coupled to what invisible body text or sentence marked by commas.

One day, I think, I will read the book of myself, that day, with my printing eyes I will pour the water of memory right on the book. That book will be my last bed, with the text lying in it: my body then like a slumber of the body of the Only Most Near man. This is what I desired: to be the immaterial production of the peace of his body, to add myself to his death, to be the rippling transparent sheet which envelops him and in the very time of weaving to dwell in the most secret part of the chest and mingled with the oldest of his desires to linger to efface myself on the endless edge of his Most Near body. To be dreamt of him as I dreamt him and just as a scene returns to my eyes so heart-rending that I still tremble and flee from it: yet it was an imaginary scene, but so beautiful in its precision, so violent and so cruel that it could not fail to be true in some organic or dramatic place, in some story known by other dreamers or lovers or dancers. I attended it, yet I felt nothing, not more in truth than if I had read what I was seeing, and perhaps therefore I was reading it and emotions were coming to me worn out by a long journey through fiction, so that I could put up with the worst. However, it was my person which first attracted me instead of the tale: delegated, I found it very hard to reach the rocky platform round which a fake city (only grooves remained and no building) deposed and that I am knowable from the point of view of the unknowable only, and coupled to what invisible body text or sentence marked by commas.

One day, I think, I will read the book of myself, that day, with my printing eyes I will pour the water of memory right on the book. That book will be my last bed, with the text lying in it: my body then like a slumber of the body of the Only Most Near man. This is what I desired: to be the immaterial production of the peace of his body, to add myself to his death, to be the rippling transparent sheet which envelops him and in the very time of weaving to dwell in the most secret part of the chest and mingled with the oldest of his desires to linger to efface myself on the endless edge of his Most Near body. To be dreamt of him as I dreamt him and just as a scene returns to my eyes so heart-rending that I still tremble and flee from it: yet it was an imaginary scene, but so beautiful in its precision, so violent and so cruel that it could not fail to be true in some organic or dramatic place, in some story known by other dreamers or lovers or dancers. I attended it, yet I felt nothing, not more in truth than if I had read what I was seeing, and perhaps therefore I was reading it and emotions were coming to me worn out by a long journey through fiction, so that I could put up with the worst. However, it was my person which first attracted me instead of the tale: delegated, I found it very hard to reach the rocky platform round which a fake city (only grooves remained and no building)

pressed its abstract form. On this stratified natural platform, brutal to any eye, with uncrossed, unthinkable,
indescribable monuments of an exemplary immediacy,
a giant eye pivoted, barring the way on the right, barring the way on the left, barring the way between the
right and the left and between left on the left methodically but also maliciously. I could not cross the bar and
I was stopped within human distance of the monument, and held back, transfixed with hatred, by the
heinous spectacle of the pivoting eye. My vital juices
were bitter. At the intersection of the monumental ban
and of a future perfect of my hatred, three weird sisters
framed young Dioniris: they were naked, they stuck to
their sacred role like a skin, they were tall, their heads
heavily crowned with grey plaits, awfully lined with
age, the sacred breasts they wore at the front of their
bodies were furrowed indented fringed by time.
Dioniris was weeping, staring wildly, letting out cries
which rasped my throat and feared being converted.
These women did not lack suppleness and at times an
appalling grace. Their initiatory gestures were so old so
slow so precise that they took on a natural force of law,
thus concealing whatever ruse and calculation there
could be in their clever contortions. I could see them
holding Dioniris by his extremities and initiating him
and from my dry throat I could draw no sound strong
enough to protest yet my rage had the strength of an
army. But I was held back by the necessity to defend
myself against the perfidious tricks of the pivoting eye,

whose threatening winks took turns with revolting slippages of codes: to the threat was added the tacit invitation to complicity, as if it were congratulating me on the sly for being the organizer or the author of this scene. It wasn't true. But it wasn't really false: I was inscribed in a luminous space from which I could no more dissociate myself than the letter can move away from the page. Thus I occupied the place of the gaze in the system of this spectacle: without me it could not have taken place but I had the powerless primordial presence of a place.

Yet conversion occurs! Dioniris dumb, still held by these beings of an unknown order, loses colour, then thickness, and, in a muffled crumpling which makes me jump, takes leaf and becomes ivy. And I would have believed I had dreamt this substitution or to read it or perhaps to have written it or to write it if I had not suffered the aftershock of this disappearance and if my kinship with the leaf had not brought about, in truth consecrated, an imminent identification. I had screamed when he was a being of flesh. Now I was torn down the middle. All that befell him could take place in my body. There was a natural relation between the scene of conversion and my eyes and the strength of my revolt and the leaf

*or T'extamant**

hear the voice of light screaming and flashing are the eyes of the twice born who prevents me from seeing: the more I want to see and focus the less I make out except for the violent ribbon which burns my eyes to their roots. Thus is inscribed the red book, through a cruel reading, it is the mythical book the one nobody writes, but which tears and blood and desire and hope throw onto marvellous flying leaves whose secret strength flares up under the gaze.

When I close my eyes to see it, around me, rivers of ashes, mountains of ashes and palaces of ashes divide and distribute themselves to infinity, where there used to be cities there are seas of ashes. Yet I do not weep for Dioniris is not dead and my eyes are bathed in memory. I myself descended into the dark coolness of the foliage. I hold in my hand not far from my eyes a mere leaf of liber, sensitive, folded, light, still wet. Another than me has held this text.

A leaf for me the same leaf for Him flares up by itself.

And not far from my eyes, it holds my hand and burns me contemporaneous and previous, my prophetic body, my body's body, my desire, my arrested source, my living tomb, my archives, this leaf, sensitive, fragrant, to be read without properly dying, to the absolute, where when what I cannot be is what I am,

I take a wand and draw on the hard sand; here I am, here was Pergamum, and all the sand supposes that it is our bed; there is the Garden. There was a tree in that garden. I draw it. This is where I saw Dioniris. A wave comes and sweeps away Pergamum, Dioniris and the tree. The sand remains.

Then I was, a human creature, in front of a Wall, the wall was manifold, each other wall was a time, and I had to go past the wall without assistance without resorting to a ladder without cunning

It is as difficult to go past this wall as for the son of myrrh not to seduce and die

One had to go past the wall or to cross it or to overcome it but without a ladder without formulae without herbs with the grace of fragrances which over-whelm gods and make possible impossible unions, but without fragrance,

the wall of walls, porphyry which cannot be crossed through strength or cunning

It is as difficult to cross a wall which is one flesh with memory,

It is as difficult to love a dead being as not to love him, and difficult too, but not impossible for Love, which compels to love whoever is loved, to compel the one who is neither on the sea, nor on the table of lands, nor among mountains, nor in any big and known city,

but lying, it is not impossible or possible, short of exit-
ing the Garden of Disappearances through the Garden
of Appearances, put a distance between gardens and
your desire, turn sharply right and equally sharply left
and equally squarely in all directions and any whatso-
ever in order to shake off with an unceasing whirling
motion the order of times rolls glides dives flies spurn-
ing land and sea, thrash about without fail, work the air
with illusions and seedlings of laughter do not rest until
you manage to make Peruvia, where Love compels
whoever is loved no matter how impossible to find he
may be in the East and in the West, to love. There
remain nothing but ruins of reason, the roar of discourse and the etymological state. There frankincense
and myrrh are secreted by one and the same trunk, and
life and death have the same smell of mint and the same
plant agitates and calms lovers.

without using my hands or feet or movements of
my body for help, I had to cross it.

this wall encountered in the biggest city was the
sum of human constructions very different from the
symbolic wall which I was building every day in order
to keep time aside very different from the walls of time
from which our race was drawing echoes of gold,

Volume without border without edge without
profile without form more wall than construction in
truth; the sum and rest of human dreams but without
accumulation,

Or: bed, standing, going over the Wall or conversely wall which turns into a bed before my entreating gaze.

In truth neither wall nor bed but either according to my weakness or my strength, and by chance or necessity according to the work of my desire, like a cosmic part detached from myself in the course of time, against which I always had to knock again, no matter which turn my life took. Wall or product of the desire to cross Self, adding up of appearances and disappearances my unfathomable parent. Between us: the opera of confrontations what is called elsewhere the war theatre, but without winner or loser except the place churned up a thousand times. I then only need to cross this unsteady construction to be on my other side. Now the wall of desire is not a true wall, that's why it is so difficult to cross, can this fabulous concretion of absences and illusions actually be crossed?

Only the being of desire which returns from a death of its own and then takes on the dangerous construction from the rear is undone from the desire for the wall and knows absolute desire, the one which creates the effect of eternity. I knew one. But I, mortal, am indissociable from the obstacle, who but for that would be as bare and weakened as a comma outside its sentence, who without this text would be as hollow and disused as a waterless seabed.

Sometimes it seemed to me that I stemmed from the wall instead of being its worker or simultaneously the work and the work's work, and that I went back

into it only to be thrown straightaway onto the future
where all thoughts being scattered I was but the dislo-
cated echo of his death. I needed years of long ceaseless
reflection to piece myself together again, to win back
one single second of the thousand I had lost and I was
pitifully afraid of remaining bogged down in this fictitious time whose strength nourished towards me the
dangerous passion of a mother for the newly born
child. And yet I was guilty of having aroused it, I was
the mother, the child and the passion, and I was the tri-
angle and the desire of its disembowelling, all at once
and mutually, aiming both at the centre and the periphery, so that, torn apart, I retraced my steps unrelentingly
but with such zealous effort that at the end of a thousand years I had reinscribed but one rare moment on
behalf of the present, if that: bloodless.

Then I had the certainty that if the wall had been
a true wall and not the stratagem of time, even very
high, I would have found the strength to leap over it
or to reduce it to my human measure and I could
already feel the form and the height of the leap regis-
tering in the play of my muscles. But it was rather the
wall of Substitutions closer in appearance to an animated canvas, painted with a thousand Subjects, such
as Dante unfolds in his bible, a wall of walls invisible to
the living, a shore inhospitable to the dead, a natural
shore, range, cliff, such as lovers walk along during their
centuries and their dreams and beyond: and each desire
increases it with a thickness, each dream troubles it with

a depth, any pleasure doubles it and it strengthens itself from any fear, but lovers' patience is infinite when clasped in an embrace they slip along their blindness, the eyes of one dazzling themselves in the eyes of the other, their tenuous dance goes over the wall by reverberation, they leave luminous trails behind their eyes and this bright canvas veils them, follows them, intrigues them and reproduces them, carries them here ties them up here, unties them, makes a loud mockery of their exchanges stages into comedy the words of one on the lips of another, and writes up their lives in echo, acts as a relay for their illusion, taking care if need be, by accident or out of calculation, to carry out the dancers' imperceptible recharge, so much so and so often that this felicitous shuttle which the tireless couple performs during the course of its story makes up the unmarked time of love, the time which does not fall within the purview of time but within that of the couple of lovers, an insulating couple and time, non-conductive of age and fear. And, in the course of centuries, it is not the couple which wears itself out it is the sense of time it is the material opposition between the lovers become love and the wall of substitutions becoming the very movement of love and thus exchanged, mobile, reversible.

See them now as they make the canvas stir whence they come, where Dante had painted them, sitting side by side, similar in each respect like siblings and lovers, with a book in their lap, trembling from reading that they have already been read, reading until after their death their first kiss now already trembling on their lips still in the book already tasted by the lips written by the one who walked-on-the-floor-of-time bewildered to read themselves already kissed already seen already separated forever reunited all shuddering from the kiss prescribed not to be laid holding in their veins the blood's race passes into the book's veins which marking them with the stamp of death marks them for life, all mixed still and since for ever, as in one single comma-less sentence the uncertain syntax brings itself at will to the uncertain edge of things, them loved by Love which compels to love whoever is loved and which presides over the destiny of whoever loves, which is neither before the lover's desire nor after, neither beside nor at the bottom and which, however, precedes follows accompanies and transports desire by leaps and bounds well beyond all times making belly and throat to memory pulling the future down to certainty, see them reading in the book open in their lap how Love, which compels to love, makes him take from him such a strong pleasure that, as you can see, he does not abandon him yet, and see also written further in the book, the one which rests in the lovers' lap and the one which rests under your eyes and the one which the One who walked-on-the-floor-of-time was writing and

If you read the book through the agency of the book which reads it if you persevere and read the book which has read the book which reads the one which lies open in the lovers' lap and if through the mediation of the book you bring yourself ever more closely, without pleasure ever expiring, to other laps which ardour still causes to shiver through the privilege of love which rules over the circle of memory, you will read then how the kiss moves from mouth to mouth and makes the canvas stir where a thousand lovers are trembling on the edge of lips so much desired.

And now lay the kiss. There where the kiss alights, take the book. And now close your eyes for a moment, let light fall and look at these who punctuate for a time the dancing wall of Substitutions, then look at the book: it's us.

This book is our etymology. Is the reading of the most precious body, which nowadays cannot be found, of this Most Near man whom I do not await whom I await on the other re-embroidered side of time. And if this book is not perfect, it's because it lacks its other books: it lacks the book which could have been the reading of the same love, but performed by it, flared up with eternity as it was, whereas this book is nothing but time and mockery for life prevents me from approaching where one dies near enough. Yet I strive and strive again, through readings delivered against the order of the possible, of sense, of history, of the compulsory inequality among the survivors and their handsome

enraptured bodies, to unread what got imprinted over
there, from the Garden of Disappearances where everything made me think of his death

so searingly that I could not hold on, for no sooner had
I made three reconnaissance movements, thinking from
the effervescence in my blood and the turmoil in my
spirits that I was no doubt approaching the vicinity of
a thought where I could think of his death, than my
imaginary vessel sank, breaking its momentum on the
very thought which I had set in front of what I was
thinking as it is so difficult for whoever is kept in a
body to think disappearance without executing themselves by disappearing from thought and simultaneously
by sinking thought by disappearing it, short of pretend-
ing to think or to disappear, therefore I was prowling
and reflecting, despairing of approaching the place from
where he, as close to death as I was close to him, had
to, I suppose, cast much more efficient and stronger
thoughts towards his proper disappearance from a bare,
hard place, without geographical place and without
root where perhaps he was already no longer in the
order of his body, a hearth without fire without air
without water without earth whose sole thought had
the power to throw my imagination into a state of allu-
sion where no thought could have stopped or been
produced, where I found myself without images, without breath, without reference, sere to the last degree, a
morbid yet poetic state strangely, which comes together

with an exhaustion of symbolic strength, I was drier than the skin of Arabian dates, my flesh sere from the proximity of disappearance, in this burning place where death is most closely joined to the driest life.

It is as difficult to forget oneself as to arrive in Peruvia. However, by dint of close contact with his immortality, I sometimes reached the edge of my oblivion, this reversible bank of history where all that is desirable is relieved by negative memory, the one which, still secret, returns from times to come.

It is possible to swim in a waterless sea if one is not afraid of the rock protruding. Flesh then attests to the crossing. Thus, being in close contact with this unexpected man's immortality, I painfully ventured to the outermost reaches of times, knowing the risk of losing my life from memory, till where images fall, threads snap, figures scatter, where air beneath the text almost no longer flows, where desire becomes its own index of eternity, pointing further and further till oblivion. One must then furnish oblivion: nobody gets near who still clings to his body. Those, among the lovers, who have almost succeeded, have let it be known to what extent bodies can be sublimated through it, under the propitious fire of oblivion, to which Love in Peruvia submits them, they take on a wrinkled aspect like a parchment, which is not without charm or gentleness (whence the fantasy of a paper being comes to me). Almost: by dint of wishing to reach the forever hidden

side of our story, I, a barren figure, attached to representing to myself the coolness of death, was coming to
a land bordering on real death, where desiring beings
are at once very powerful and very frail, in the fashion
of gods and moons eclipsed by too bright a daylight
and of over-exposed humans. He, in the middle of a
contemporary story and a stone's throw away from the
golden heart of the West, could push back matter and
its laws, perforate through suggestion the face of destiny
and, through the hole thus made, flow from one edge
of time to the other. With a passionate eye push back
through insistence and pressure the oldest mountains;
through the concentration of desire into one single
point, dissolve its ban; and in the same stroke brave my
haunted time with his present, grant what would be to
what could have been through clever splices. *He*
(Dioniris) was himself that wall against which he was
standing out, where he was embedded, which
obstructed me, which was inseparable from us and
independent from us: neither painting, nor handwriting, nor stylus, nor hammer, nor chisel, nothing had a
hold on this substance, familiar in the long run and
imperative. But insuperable. If I'd had other eyes to read
him I could have reproduced his secret ink, *Tombe*
would not have lacked the book in the place of which
this one is being written. But if I had known why
Tombe is being written and not the other one, I would
not have had the desire or the obligation to return to
this wall to the point of delirium. All the delusions and

all the cautions and all the wiles of conservation had settled there.

That's why this book lacks the book of death, which this book is only a parody of. But this book does not come far from the book of death, and at times even brushes against it. And my body in its bed was very close to death, and in its revolutions this bed came within distance of the Sex of Gold which I could see shining in full light. When we were lying side by side, on the earth, on the grass, on a carpet, on an animal's skin, it was enough for us to imagine the Sex of Gold together, and the image went to our heads, then we were blasted by a gigantic explosion.

Let's make no mistake about it: this strange, terrible story is not mine, others in other names have been subjected to it, and I had already read it a hundred times. That's why, having these readings, this memory, and this terror, I tried to divert its course and counter-write it:

attempt now to pull the top to the bottom

and once again attempt to make the East coincide with the West: an undertaking as absurd but as exhilarating as to make being say that it is not.

Nearer the top than the bottom, where the biggest birds make up their cinnamomum nests out of reach, we had a dizzying, almost inaccessible lodging. Everything in that place made life difficult, in particular the necessary climb. We were young and vigorous, heavy and light. I did not fear exertion but I was loath to step into what made me think of a chest. *He*, (Dioniris), did not hesitate: Would you fancy living in a room as small as a casket which would be located at the top of a hotel which one would reach from the outside wall of the building, and without assistance? I had to climb first, he was following me. The climb, however, was made easier by the fact that some cavities were hollowed out at regular intervals where the tip of the foot would fit. We hoisted ourselves up, we then had to squeeze through a very narrow, rectangular opening, and, in this library, I could touch live with my fingers the mythologies, the sacred texts, the medical sciences, the stories of origins, the archives of modern as well as ancient massacres, the jumble of memory fattened by death, the cinnamon rolls, the feathers of unalterable eagles, the sap of myrrh and the balls of frankincense, and all the books so fragrant and so alive in the chest from above that it was impossible to disentangle their smell from the one, so wild and suave, that was given off by Dioniris' mouth and his most warm and dry body not far from my eagerness. I was suffocating; thus in the chink of times on this side of memory and not far from culture, we were possessed by pleasure.

Our lodging had a low ceiling yet its space was flexible and confined like the text of the Vedas: the sky reflected us to the ground which reflected us to the sky all the time. Small investments small outlays small suffocations. I felt nostalgic about the Garden of

Disappearances and the big leaps of squirrels and about the forks and junctions and shivers of leaves and about the fine swing of very tall trees. Our casket was limited, drawn with a ruler, narrow, cutting, so much that one ran the risk of death by suffocation. When one was outside, it was sunk in the wall to such an extent that one could not see it, when one was inside one could no longer see the sky and this non-seeing was as strong as if the sky had never been: the sky was not. And the non-seeing was not nor any seeing and the inside was not nor the inside and we vegetated among the fragrances as the gods vegetate who neither are nor are not. There was this smell. And without further ado we were caught up by absence and lay intestate among those books, on cinnamon rolls, contaminated by the root, by what from us was brought down or buried, recumbent bodies amid recumbent letters, sheltered from storms, but devoured. We staggered out of there in extremis dazzled then I was throbbing with impatience and with doubt: Were we right to live under this arch and to restrict ourselves was I incapable of sublime economy could I not live off the fragrance of this Most precious body, did I need the empire of airs and the kingdom of eyes in order to sate my coarse appetites was I loved by an indestructible god or destroyed by a divine love to what noble or ignoble distance from the known were we lying and when we slept up there was it the same sleep which was waking us, did we with closed eyes each come under the same authority, were

we given back to the same surface would we then have
written the same book or would we have read this
same story in the same tone of voice? I saw us to be
similar to two venomous syntagms joined but held
apart by a copula as in the sentence Dioniris/is/here
which I repeated to myself while falling asleep and
awakening and which kept away precisely through this
ambiguous coitus too pressing a presence. Likewise
when the gay voice rebuked me with a *You/are/there* I
suspected without saying so my Most Near and Most
Young beloved of making sure that I was not too much
there but I refrained from putting the meaning to the
test, finding advantages, my security and my secret
pleasure in these shadows which made sentences topple
and my desire swerve from either edge.

A QUESTION OF AGE OR OF EPOCH:

What age was he when all was suspended on time
which numbered the days for him is impossible to say,
for there was no more key of time then, nor box nor
chest nor quantity but superb and staggering effects of
time, according to whether I feared or hoped he was
young extremely and even to the point of infancy and
He himself seemed on the spot to be already well
advanced in his Story, through the passion of my eyes
now he appeared in the mortal coat, now so powerful
and venerable that it seemed to me not that I saw him
with my mortal eyes but that I knew him as in a dream

one knows and sees the one whom one has never seen who seen in a dream is the one whom one had always wanted to see, that the dream effaces as it fades, that the bitter night carries away, leaving in the dream's place nothing but the gentle impression which was born of it, it seemed to me then that I was the place where his story rang loud and at times the memory which invented it, the light which came from him in order to reflect back on him, ever since the most ancient times: he then had the age of The One who leans back against the work of a whole life, so that I felt traversed, foreseen, suppressed, loved in anticipation and always anticipated.

The more I knew him the less I knew him, the nearer I drew the less I came near him, the more I desired him the less I hoped for him.

Yet he was still very near my body, and from my knowledge still very far.

When I saw him sleeping, I was almost sure he would never grow old: he had the smooth transparent face of a very young man who still sleeps close to the sourmother's fragrance, with adolescent features, his lids calm as of somebody who is not afraid of awakening, his forehead so white that it accentuated the darkness of mine, and a light so pure came from his cheeks that I understood how one can speak of 'source' for light, of flood, of bath, that I had a perpetual thirst for it and that my tongue and my eyes mixed up their desires: his eyes his mouths for my mouth his forehead a water so limpid that its bottom was its surface and that leaning over its expanse the features of my face were reflected back and faintly struck the pupils of my eyes.

What age was Achilles when he loved Patroclus dead more than Achilles' life, the age of eternity? What age? and what age Adonis too young for Love when he was loved too much? And he neither mortal nor non-mortal when he made me know what comes from the dead to the living just as Love makes men know what comes from the gods, He neither young nor old but aged and like the ageing eagle already new and with an igneous body,

If ages had depths, I would have loved him from the depths of Ages and also as and when he was produced by ages, and as and when I was produced by other ages or his.

I loved him from the depth of ages and from the domed roofs of Peruvia's round square flattened swollen houses and from the erect roofs of the buildings of Pergamum. With arms stretched high up, towards the Most High he seemed to me to be, but sometimes head down as well, burrowing in the earth where I thought he was rooted,

I loved him from the edges of perused books, from their uncertain margins, from all the tales of love and absence.

But in truth still today

Centuries after his death I love him from the edge to the centre of my body and I love him from and to the centre's centre, the eye of my belly

As and when he produces by my life and by his death in my life a living love, a still new love yet the oldest, the first one

From my navel through my belly via a fantastical network of knotted snares and threads and knots which can and cannot be untied all the way to his navel and in truth this very day I can feel him moving in my belly and weeping in my throat like yester eve. And I write this book from the depth of him, with the pen which I had thrust gently into his anus. The entrance—or the exit—of his body was narrow and thin as of a child the sweet entrance and the secret white throat at bedtime at the base of the gentle throbbing cradles, I had wanted the nib to have been in him, in those days less sad than these days when in its golden horror Pergamum was shining from seeing us walking alive between its flanks, and now here in my clenched hand the same but naked pen cutting uncovered in order to pierce the unpierce-able time, mad, stiff, uncapped, absurd and staggering, cleaving from a long-charred tree, desire of an impos-sible cleft doubled loss, lost losing never losing enough except soon, when at last I have lain down alongside the text which I am laying down, at this moment when I am still unique and without reflection, alongside this Most Near body which my body was encompassing

What age was Time when it produced the encounter: a great age and an age of birth, his age and our non-age, as well as an age with two tips, the one through which the semifather could be the sourmother for his son, the other through which the son would be for his semifather the woman through whom both would have passed. Thus He, through the body which I was making for myself by dint of loving him and getting near him, such as I could see him with the blind yet infallible eye which marks the centre of my body, was young, not yet born or already returned, I his wet and delicate tomb, and his child, and I our child, and he more than once born.

When one makes love from eye to eye, the lower eyelashes mingled the upper lashes embraced, with irides giant and hazy, on the iridescent surface is born a minute film of tears which are not salted, but lukewarm and soft, fluid and brisk like mercury, which pass from one duct to the other and there, from one conjunctiva to the other as if the eye-to-eye were one single eye with two sides, a continuous eye or an eye-within-an-eye. We made that love once only, bodies were overturned, the tips of his feet eastwards, the tips of my feet westwards, his left cheek against my left cheek, my eyelashes woven of his own, and I could see his dazzling eye, brown or golden, I think, filling in the space of my eye; this blind love eye to eye leaves one unsatisfied, fascinates, subjugates and flees, like love from tongue to tongue and all the kinds of union through the surface: they lack the hole, the tomb, the fall. But there is this strange secretion, these tears, this phlogistic: what the eye thus dazzled sees, which, without making one fall, yet enraptures, is what the gold embryo sees when it is neither man nor woman yet but already and for ever the simulacrum of the Sex of Gold, and when it is bathed in frankincense.

Of what is Love love of: Of what it is deprived? It will be as with the hunter in love with wild doves.

Build a dovecote or suppose it's all built. It is difficult to capture wild doves alive but it's not impossible. It's not impossible for her, the lover to capture the wild beloved but it is almost impossible.

O mint and you brown myrtle receive him without bruising him when he falls! When my desire has laid him down perfume him and keep him for my desire. I will have neither rest nor peace until I have brought him down towards me from the top of his perse sky as does the bird-catcher in love with the bird and the mad hunter with the wild dove.

What if one is no longer deprived? If one lacks the lack in which Love does its feathers?

Build the dovecote first. Then capture wild doves alive or such another bird or wryneck or eagle from above which defies hunting and now rejoice for you possess the living birds and you can breed them in your dovecote. And now you are in possession of your wild doves. But in another sense you don't have a single one of these wild doves which you now have within reach which if they are in the cage within your reach are graspable and not wild.

Instead of the dove represent the beloved who once caught is shut up by the loving woman within the enclosure of Love: and represent the question of Love. And now that you possess and hold back the dove which is neither wild nor familiar, release it if you want to have it

Release it

It is one thing to possess the Beloved, another thing to have him. But when I see him lying, felled to the ground, with his wings folded and eyelids shut, but without trace without wound without crumpling still virgin and on the ground apparently lifeless three times more beautiful than me,
Then I will wish to have him;
no sooner will I have seen him lying,
than the hunt starts again,
Do I have him?
Desire, invent the resource   of detachment which keeps the Desired one alive!
Let an endless possibility suddenly happen to catch to hold the one who is within the enclosure of Love and the same possibility to miss him to release him and to desire him, as many times as desire desires until the dovecote becomes wild

Containing still wild doves, birds of different kinds, instead of birds desiring beings, lovers always agitated, brisk beloveds who flutter about on their own, as it happens, through all the others, or the squirrel.

There he is! Who? Him! Who else but him? There He is, running a gold point through the text and tearing it! Which mesh, which hands could hold him back! And now that Love has let fly this strange dart at me, with what laughter will I be able to laugh?

There he is, looking like nobody,

It is not inconceivable for a squirrel to be enamoured of a young woman, but who knows the fantasies and follies of a squirrel? Perhaps they are powerful and refined, perhaps gentle and skilful and marvellously brutal. Imagine a young woman's passion for a squirrel. Such a passion ran through me with a vivid, natural movement some night in the high library. I was then as innocent as a sheet of paper threatened with ink, still without a heading, a free shaving, a sheet similar to itself divine by its two sides virgin without history but rich in virtualities. I was graspable in all senses.

The hunter captive of the spirit of the hunt.

A gold shaft   runs through what is my improper Brusque body, a Leaping form. And I, pure acceptance without motive without memory without project without need pure out-of-body product of a sequence of three beats, here I am soon, a sentence set down through three beats of which I was but the burning circumstance, combustible also combustion, by the grace of three leaps from an Unexpected squirrel, in a gold fur, in the thick of the night but which did not harm my eyesight, I saw a Squirrel, I saw him, I wanted him, I want him

With a leap, Desire in one fell stroke goes off through the air in the thick of the night. There I see: our bodies lying under the perse arch glow astral among the sacred volumes motionless but for the stroke already gone off. A body goes and crosses this glowing body near Dioniris' body which soon no doubt will be mine, an ahead of myself loving, my presence here there and there irresistibly,

A stroke: and a strength to demand myself still on this side of time, irrevocable stroke of force, as the law of Him inscribes in the perse air cleft around us the Unexpected and its advance.

All, from now on, will be in advance: I surrender, barely surrendered, I get ahead of myself, thus a perilous game in turns and at the same time on my guard and already turned forced but in the vanguard I am taken and I take in succession

And at the same time already invested I invest this body by force and call it what it will be in advance: Desire

No sooner desired no longer fears attrition: gone off at a stroke under the arch and with a gold body through the body which would be mine and gold, the inconceivable flesh is made which never alters, a dough

where eternal flours mingle, and here is the Other, here
in those days

One night before my memory . . .

And there were on lands nothing but gardens, men
without eyes,

sexes without bodies, and Others, then in one fell
stroke: the Squirrel.

(Then it was eternity . . .

there would have been an inconceivable time before
time, there would have been this inconceivable begetting which works against bloods, whereby History is
the daughter of Memory and Memory is daughter of
History)

Then in one stroke of History and its cuts and its
slippages.

Thus barely brought into the world I had to bring
a world into the world,

A dream which was waiting for me to dream it,

however, was dreaming me,

That was how under the library arch Love made
light of mine Desire and of Desire of me, by the grace
and leap of a Squirrel, abrupt, opening, the out-scene
[*d'hors*]★

The play of forces of Love sent me back from body
to body and threw me from top to bottom, with outstretched arms open like lips and the eagerness of the
Eye riveted to the blinding rose was no less great than
my eagerness to chase the Squirrel,

Until a second time when my body took shape enough to know myself to be made the place for impulses and fires without any other referent than my own irradiation, moon with a moonlike heart,

A leaf turned back on its paper sucking it imprinting itself producing through rubbing an invisible yet inflamed text, in this surprise flame writhing, devoured yet reappearing, thus myself in a rout of any calculation ready to open to the One who Leaps-on-the-floor-of-airs, ready to make a tree for him from my bones, in my lust-for-Him-alive, the Squirrel, I am this Lust in one fell stroke, my body rising under the effect, my body-alive-with-lust [*corps-envie*]★ for this living object identifiable precisely by this swelling this levitation, by this severing of darkness by the object which suddenly created a vacuum where I lay in the thick of time by the grace and the strength and the defect of the Object of gold the one without eyes whose sex is indifferent and made of the other scene the very scene which in three leaps the squirrel planted,

In perse night, shadow of shadow, and our bodies lying among the remains and memories and among the wisdoms and jumbles.

Ruins among ruins,

A shot of life: a hard soft bullet in a silk cocoon, as a bird would wrench itself from a subterranean nest in a fallout of feathers, shatters the shadow drawn from darkness.

There's the Other!

No sooner has the Unexpected squirrel popped up, the world skips a square. Love pierces me in the neck in the palms in the navel through which Desire streams—this squirrel blinds me in the eye of my Belly. I shout very loud to Dioniris: 'Catch it O god catch it'

I sit down in darkness I shout to Dioniris: 'Catch, Raise your hand Catch catch this bird for me this object this child who scampers away in gold shafts between our bodies outside us!'

Which bird or which squirrel has grasped us in a fall-out of feathers or nameless stars come from below and of commas

And
now
no more   , , , , , ,
full stop   ! A squirrel !
but
just   , , , , , ,
a
story   *Desire*!
of commas

Is what has not been, which can no longer not be. How had it come there, in this library so high, so modern, yet so old and so far from Nature? It could have gone out of the wall, perhaps the wall had secreted it, the wall was grey rough opaque a sorry sight and thick to the touch, perhaps it was a fake squirrel, a wall squirrel, a book squirrel, some library fetish, but I was the true, the unique and the definitive desire for the squirrel, and that's why I begged Dioniris to catch it, with outstretched arms, my body raised, my fingers open. I was this need of Him. And the Universe, its peoples, its debates, its massacres: belly and hands and hole of the body of Lust and sex where to hold back the squirrel; and the sheets of air and sea sewn together with perse thread in order to make a sack where to trap the squirrel; and my name: Lust for the Squirrel; and this name: the abdominal lining of what lies in store for us.

But perhaps he had come out of Dioniris' body, perhaps it was his only son or another son whom I did not know or an excretion. I had not seen it as it went out but only when it crumbled in the stale air. How I wanted it! 'Dioniris raise your hand!' He raises his hand in order to grasp. 'Catch it and I won't fear anything any longer in the world! Put your hand on it! To please me!' Then He has it.

Invent

Another thing is to have it and we have it. He palms it off on me in the hollow of my hands. If I had a son, I would give him to him, but which son, Dioniris hands it on to me, I keep it, gently. I am afraid of hurting it, but it looks like it accepts my fingers. I caress it slowly, I feel its body in my hand, I am myself in my hand, a small body between my fingers and yet ungraspable. *Another thing is to possess.* Do I have it and now that I have it, where is it?

I will no longer be able to see it: I have it. If I open my fingers it will leap flee I keep it, I touch it I make for myself an eye which does not see but throbs and blinks in the palm of my hand, its hair was grey and white and gold and soft, I would have lived badly if Dioniris had not grasped it but now, how to live?

the resource

It was a squirrel from here, with gold hair, and I remember it had no tail when it had sprung up out of us from the unique depth of ages. Or else its body was its tail, it was made up of one single piece and I desired it throughout all my history until my death and until my sporadic dust. How from now on would I dare open this hand which had held it, which held it, holds it, which it was using in this moment as an external body. It was not strange that the minute object which was kept prisoner was my master: it was so, absolutely. And I needed it, its life, its fragility in its omnipotence. If I release it I am lost its flight ravishes meaning from me if I keep it I lose it: in my soft ardent fingers it will not find food. If I keep it I don't see it, if I see it I don't have it, it never stops perishing and I miss it ceaselessly. A unique moment among times, I have seen-held-known it and we were gods. It was not surprising for my hand to hold my whole life in its closed grasp. This squirrel had to have another name and another body, but it was the very Defect of my story, or the cherished yet terribly free body of my misfortune. I say to Dioniris: 'You have given me this misfortune which I had always sought. It is evasive and ungraspable but you have grasped it so I can see it more and to give me this pleasure. My hand was full of life. What if I opened it? Why does what I have in my hand touch what there is in my story. Why would I want to keep it not want to lose it Why?'

of the detachment which keeps

So that loss be mine. This very small squirrel, however, is very big, it is bigger than me, it is as big as Dioniris through my eyes, who in my hand is fragile, unpredictable and terrible. What if I separated my hand from my body? In a short while this hand would be open or closed, it's impossible for me to predict it. My motionless hand feels the secret motion of the squirrel; it is full of its energy, it weighs down on its lightness. If I carried it to my mouth, if I licked it and knew it with my tongue, if I swallowed it, it can happen I am wary of myself like the plague. On my closed hand a strange fire erupts, and I suffer. I so much wanted to have it and now who could I palm it off to? The hand suffers, its passion begins. Desire must invent the ruse of detachment which keeps alive the Desired One; then the dovecote becomes wild, the enclosure of Love catches fire and the consumed hand lets go. Thus the hand infected by insidious Desire: it lets go.

alive

There it is! It springs up, I see it, it's another, there it is, it's the One, without a tail, but without fur as well. It used to be covered with a gold fur. Remains the colour without the hair. It is naked but still grey, white and gold, and still young and vigorous. Doubtless it is now more fragile, is it my mistake and there is a mistake or on the contrary I should rejoice of this mortal virtue through which I am brought closer to Dioniris? The eruption reaches my arm and spreads to the shoulder. It makes its nest in a hole in the wall, it is soft but energetic, the wall has the hardness the rough ugliness and the reticence of a wall, but weakness is stronger than the strength of the wall, and the water is stronger than the rock, all wears out, I too wear out, my body shows signs of it, it is worn out too, but Nature guides it, it will break through.

I turn my head, no sooner have I turned my head than the Story takes a colossal leap backwards, a mysterious mode of production which mixes begetting and work on the wall: He, the squirrel—was there ever a time when I did not desire him—is now in a third epoch and I must have been absent—I did not move, I never stopped searching and willing, I slipped, I look at myself, I did not slip, I've always known him, I knew him already before knowing so, it was the one I knew—I averted one single gaze in order to put him

on my hand, there was an unexpected mark there, I
don't know it, I don't want it, I barely delay—I return,
I never left,—and now in a third epoch, suddenly:

Suddenly,   *the Desired One*!

there is this legend in the wall which surprises
me, I had not noticed it, yet it is fresh and bright and
clear and endlessly long, a sign that she has recently
risen from the dark foundations, and who knows what
happens beneath our bodies in connection with the
burning, then cooled matter of the universe. The crack
is fine and beautiful, cool lips of the wall so old and
sere. This is where my Most Expected love has nestled,
in the minute hollow which splits the wall from the
cement to infinity, approximately level with my belly, I
can barely find him again. In this unforeseen time, the
third one in our story, it is tiny: a larva-squirrel, almost
a worm, a bare comma. I see it with a third eye which
blinks in the middle of my belly's shield, but nothing
now proves to me that this larva-squirrel is my flying
squirrel. This one, minute, is golden, naked, extremely
fragile, motionless, a mark on the breathless leaden grey
wall,

And suddenly the enclosure of Love sways, the
doves have flown and the desperate bird-catcher dashes
forward, and rage and terror flit about in his soul; the
hand which caressed, the fingers which wove the

adored epiderm with caresses, their flesh is dry and on the flesh the rough grey bark is infected with golds. The past subsides onto the future. My right one is sere but heavy and mineral and monstrous in my eyes. If I took the Infinitely Small between these deadly fingers, would I kill it? At least if my hand had been struck by the very one it was holding naked hairless tailless but marvellously soft and mobile still a short while ago in the second time when I was still strong and pierced with desires? Or if it had been brought into the world by the second squirrel, it would be more fragile, but it would be promised to a fourth or to a second time and I could hope to see it grow, to be covered with a white and grey-coloured fur and later produce a tail at last, in a supernatural excess. Or if I am still alive, in what age? I will know it, a laughter will divide me, I will know, then I will live, then I will have no more life. Or if Nothing happened, if all fled, if my story was simply a time ripped by the invisible hole from which my life would escape★ and if *I* was the hole. Then Dioniris would be the edge from which I would fall into my dizziness, the eyelid of my blinding, the desire of book of my silence, and the layer of books the sublime excretion of my illusion of time, and my life simply the narrative of my life, and I the fragile, perishable product of this narrative, a system of sentences pinned after a fashion on this notebook by commas, squirrels, full of little rods, of threads, of marks inscribed by the Other. Or if I believe I live as I desire to live so much, but I am perhaps nothing but the body that Desire invents for itself, a prey and product of its Desire, I who am desired by this desire. And Dioniris: the name of all my desires and at the same time their completion. Dioniris laughing, me to Him given over, he Dioniris, among the books and nests of squirrels, laughing, and I threatened.

There's a story, and the path of texts, and for the future, whence we return there are these beds of squirrels, and in this stunning place, a chest which protects us, to make death is the impatience to make love and to make love is to return from among times along the terrible path where all is lack except the path and the lack.

'Which way do you go past me not to find me?' said Dioniris. He Dioniris said: 'If you were looking for me, you would find me.' Am I looking for him, have I looked for him on which path.

Many times even, I would have seen his disappearance from the garden of the living with joy; but I knew very well on the other hand that if that occurred I would be even more struck. Hasn't he struck me? Hasn't he threatened me? Hasn't he broken me? Let him come! Let him strike me! Let him smash my bosom savagely so that his name be no longer murmured! Let his death kill me so that his death be no longer mourned,

But oh the crushing weight of history, for you are gone. You are gone, never to return, and where was I when the cruel chest closed on Dioniris, where was I and if I had been there, where would I be and he?

these beds of leaves our archives—his very gentle look— if you look for me you won't find me, and now, very gentle and threatening—why do you think I am going to be dead and why do you give my body over to this thought?—very gentle threatening and fraught with prediction—under his eyes how not to lose one's hand, one's arm, one's heart and all one's body behind them, runaway, I am wary, I am wary of my body like the plague of its symptoms of its slowness of its stratagems,

why do you think I will be dead, you know me, what have you done with my body? I had warned you, why have you forsaken me?

As if he were smashing my bosom savagely so that his name be no longer caressed,

Haven't I heard you?

Haven't I adored your doors, haven't I inhabited your chest

with you?

Haven't I composed my features for you

Nothing beautiful that I forgot to do for you

Haven't I loved what is hateful

I put my left hand at your service

I dragged myself on your burning paths

Who are you that strikes me with your death?

I remember the squirrel of the first time: then I was innocent, I could think no more than a free leaf of paper, I preceded without predicting, I desired without calculating, without fearing, without hating, without straying from my desire even by a comma without turning round

It was an altogether other time, a time from before time or form after when I could desire in full life without life veiling my desire and without my desire gutting my life, not far from here in space, it was a few centuries of pain away I remember that I did not think about death for all was pursuit and movement and in front

and now I fell back into the hole of memory where all that is alive is already dead, where what is lacking has always stopped lacking, where all is cinders and no trace of fire, where my body is wrapped in a leaden skin on which death has no grip and my blackened body does not live, where I am without strength but without weakness where I read but am without voice where I do not want not to will where I do not want not to will not to will

He, Dioniris has said: 'Do not kill me'

How would I have killed life itself? and my life, how would I have killed it? 'Ah,' I exclaimed, 'this sentence kills me!' Am I death and the tomb? This sentence kills me. 'And now today he is decomposed' 'And then he was still alive' and I remember that I then thought that I would then think that I was still able to think that he was alive, but today here for three years or thirty or a thousand he has been decomposed. But what he has said is written, 'Do not kill me', and this sentence returns, returns, returns and kills me, I who have crossed deaths and travel such a long way of texts so that his word may return.

I had said: 'I will look for a way . . .' And I look for a way of looking for myself.

He will be dead. Then he will be dead. Then he is dead. Then He is no longer dead, he is no longer there he is here where I make being he expects me where I am expected, I thought that legibly. Mortal! Mortal! I have known the omnipotence of Love: I could kill him. Many times even I have thought of his disappearance with joy. Then his death would have disheartened me. I couldn't but kill him. It may have been said to me:

'Why do you think that I will be dead?

'Why do you give my body to this thought
'I see my corpse on your bed of memory
'Why do you want to lay me down
'Didn't I stay among the living
'Haven't I laid you down among my books
'I give you the future today
'Am I not a mother for you
'Why do you push me among the dead?

It is to me that he has spoken. His gaze looks at me with the threatening gentleness of the Most Far Most Near; it is me under this adored gaze who trembles, it is my eyelids that fall, it is my hands and shoulders that blacken, my whole body which spurns me with disgust, my flesh despises me and moves away in patches from my bones, my sinister neck no longer holds the head where this crime was thought. If I am the place of this thought then who am I, under the gaze of the One who can-walk-on-my-bones, who am I, blackened occupied by what kills me, me in whom the mortal sentence writes itself? Then I no longer want to be born. Let me be brought backwards.

I have known this deadly time when I had to cut through the dreaded body of the Only One in order to conceal myself in mine where wanting to live made me feel like dying and I could not die without killing him where my skin refused me and lead weighed less than my flesh, and in order to think about life I first had to have lost it. I have known this time I have not lived it, time was motionless, and I threw myself onto its walls more than ten thousand times and I covered them with blood.

If I am afraid of the one I love because he frightens me, or because I love him

fear	love	truth	the present	presence	him
and	and	and		and	and

are in league, I come to him only through the immense red silk which fear and love stretch across us.

He from the highest heights, now perched on the highest peak of Pergamum and leaping above the narrow gully with a squirrel's unpredictable briskness enjoining me to raise myself up to him erect invisible draped in veils of mist at the top of mountains produced by him, Dioniris, blurred monuments produced by the movement of his ascent, whence He was looking at me, seeing me from the top to the bottom of my story,

What have you done with my body
I say to you, Hear me, hear me, I do not bend
I do not enter your house
You are in this house which I do not know
Who speaks to you therein
I told you I was waiting for you outside,
You have invited me into this house and I have seen something which is mortal
You, come and meet up with me
I say to you again: Meet up with me outside
If all of a sudden I was going to be caught over there down below
I must question you
There will be all the questions, no matter which
This thought, this house
All the questions will be of the police type.
The zone will be cleaned up.
Which house which thought
I told you, keep me, haven't I told you
I told you don't expose me

You let somebody enter your house
Am I not faithful to my resolution
The coldest and the most implacable
You know me
What have you done with my name
What I had given I take it back,
If you want to take it back
Go up

diving from the top of his personal edifices, which reached me off-guard and transported me with a desirable horror. In order to know who I am for him, I must climb up there. I have not learnt how to climb, one must invent everything, I look for gestures of climbing in my limbs. I could have met up with him going by sea if it had not been dangerous and too long: How many years indeed to sail past those narrow straits now deserted by waters and harrowing now overflowing and so close to the ceiling that I risk dying of suffocation from swimming there, now troubled and crisscrossed with snakes and pipes mingled with excrements with silt with the flotsam and jetsam of nations, now of a depth unbearable to the imagination and so terrible that it was depicted on the very surface and gripped all muscles? If however I had been able to cross the range of Seas I would have arrived too late and blind torn to shreds, worn out, fringed gashed shapeless and repulsive to his adored gaze. And He may be dead meanwhile: bigger then, more unpredictable and threatening, more the Other than ever when he was not yet dead. Then he would be unkillable. And I would be forever shifting, tucked in my swaddling clothes of death and never dead, bound only in fine veils of illusion.

From the highest point of the highest mountain which his omnipotence ascended while piling up traces of life and traces of death plugged with gold and with excrements from all nations, he summoned me to show myself to his naked eyes. I could not hear well. Yet I grasped every word and sentences in their entirety— these are sentences which come back by themselves through the centuries from his death and nothing neither seas nor others nor walls can stop them—but (and my story would have nothing strikingly distinctive without this decisively important detail) when the words 'I can see you' or 'Do not kill me' crossed the space, whether he was quite close or very distant, they reached me such as He, Dioniris had uttered them, and yet at the same instant I sensed an almost imperceptible muffling of tones, I had the impression that each word had been taken to one side, wrapped up soundproofed then put back in place in the syntagm which reached my ears in the guise of a reconstituted sentence, of a composition made up of isolated elements, true I was wary of my ears like the plague, I had thought indeed that this veil was perhaps stretched by my hearing or by some unheard-of defect, but I checked that this phenomenon occurred only for the same well-known

sentences well listened to and precisely the most felicitous; those which spoke of survival, which announced
the union and which allow victory over time and more
clearly still those which gave an account of our future
wedding after the death of his death. Those sentences
which predicted life reached me in the wrappings of
death, their meaning preserved, their appearance preserved, the voice painted on their envelope was the
voice of the one who is still speaking to me with this
voice across times. I was cruelly sure that this tissue,
imperceptible except to my ears, was the insinuating
epigraph of his death but I was not really sure. I had no
other proof than my misfortune for He, Dioniris,
seemed not to feel this alteration, so that I had to be
suspicious of myself. I listened to myself listening, I
watched myself, I stretched my neck, I received each
word with a precision never reached by a human being,
I split these short but precious texts which closed on
themselves naturally, I was suffused borne rolled lifted
put down to his liking, I was at the mercy of his varia-
tions I sank or sprang up according to whether it
swamped or lulled me, and never did I manage to hear
it at its source. He, Dioniris, spoke but it was the voice
which I heard. O my love my love did he know what
the voice which had issued from his throat gave my ears
to hear. This imperceptible thing in itself alluringly gentle which wounded my ear without touching me and
of such a peculiar delicacy that it bristled my skin, was
he the author thereof but then why not say so and did

he wish to hide the echo from me, or did he want to feel to the limit the subtlety of my attention, and what was expected of me, did I have to tear or to let myself be taken or to send back what was untearable and ungraspable for me. What if the veil had not issued from Him, Dioniris, but was produced perhaps by some mysterious membrane harbinger of death similar to those membranes which I sometimes find in my throat after a dream of mourning and which only a ringing laughter could dissolve, did I have to tell him I was afraid and could he laugh about death till expiry? What if this veil was a trick of fear to which Love sent me back and what if this veil was in my ears the clenching of time, or perhaps the amorous fabric in whose folds I cloaked my rage.

If I had known that he was eternal and if I had been eternal, would I have desired the wedding? And would he have married me for life or did he want to marry me against death? I asked those questions like traps, at the most accessible edge; when we came back from among dreams, before or after this time, and still voiceless, in this time and without fear when I could love him alive or dead and without fearing him

Before a thousand days where will we be. I would like to ask Dioniris this question but there is no place where to ask it. Dioniris has no time to be elsewhere than in the moment when all the lives come to him, so that it would take him a thousand times for each hour to begin to dominate the monumental present, and even if Dioniris had the time to think beforehand would I ask this question or would I ask the question which it carries and which carries it, and which woman would ask the question which, if asked, kills the one, the Only One, who knows how to answer. Where, then, shall I rest, I who am hunted by the present? I will die of regret for I am born in the grave of the Only One who brings me into the world.

There he is!
He is not dead. He is standing. There he is!
How would I wake up without going through his body
I chase this body which escapes me
I want that Other one no other one to go
without the Other through whom one must go
Vein to vein and breath to breath in Extreme Proximity
Born buried between Dioniris and the one he is for me-his-Image-of-Love
Lost broken reappearing I describe the one who loses me
With thirty tears at the severed joints of my whole
My blood escapes and flows down to the stock
I am the rejected body of his body through which the same blood flows back up
Whom would I hate whom would I stop hating whom today would I love if I was sure that he was dead

Who, if I was not dead from his death, would lead
me to kill
In whom would I find death, in whom my story,
in which story my meaning and this oriented fluid
through which I flow across time?
I dig two holes beneath the seas the other to lose
myself the one to hurl him towards it
But after me the other blocks them, I have no way
behind, I have no way forward I must dig a hole
beneath the seas for myself

I build a castle on the seas each wall I double with
four walls waters are forbidden I make my bed in this
castle I believe myself to be strong I put myself in its
trust I lie down in it. But always the blow comes where
I do not expect it and the one submerges the Other

I gaze at his face night and day I hold his face in
the grip of my eyes I double each breath of his with
one of mine and I work relentlessly I secrete a thread
with my nerves each millimetre of this thread wears me
down to the heart but I move forward and I display a
unique capacity for work stitch after stitch I sew and
create the being who cannot not be, this creation is
infinite but always the blow comes where it is not
anticipated I believe him to be strong and suddenly
He tears *himself*
And my body is empty right down to the heart

And now you're gone, and now you're gone but I
don't weep
Where has he been when he was asleep, I saw his
insane body sleeping
He did not throw himself towards me this morning
I ran towards him I walked beside him I watched
him walking. He found it hard to see me
His young body rejects me
He says that he knows his body, I believe him, he
knows what he is saying I don't believe him
He says that he has no formulated thoughts but
that all that is thought will eventually be said;
His body, insane, thus god

His body writes itself on him: What bond is there
between paper and handwriting, between the still
free ream of paper, the paper knife, handwriting,
the hand which writes the blood in the hand and
what is written
What bond of hatred of kinship of sense of production of temporality between the leaf the notebook the ream the creamy white and what is
written
; and what is written
and my eye
Of sense of obligation of obedience of possession
between the blood red, the blue black and the
white—but I did not choose my blood and signs

He was not in his body this morning, something in him hates me from very far without daring to hate me and hates me for not saying so. He does not think so.

He says that he was looking for me. I'm the one who found him.

He sucks in his lips he turns away from my body. He makes me ashamed

He did not laugh this morning and he saw me looking for him

There is something other in him that I don't know With which I have no bond. An undesirable evil There will be no more future in the future But all is known beforehand

He says that he was not afraid of loving me: I was afraid, I fled, I fled towards him, I am afraid

He entered the air this morning without me

He was swimming vigorously in this most deep, withheld freezing air

When he emerges his body is shining and I run towards him as if he were new. But no sooner have I taken three leaps in order to throw myself towards him and I thus got nearer the Most Near than I do not see him any more he has vanished into thin air as do these shadows from Hell; then my open arms break and split and fall into ashes, one half of my body burns the other one.

It is Him, Dioniris, who picks me up, and laughs at last. This laughter lifts a corner of the veil, I see myself a hundredth of a second and here is what is apparent:

I threw myself towards him, Dioniris, real, alive, my impetus aimed at him, I crossed a couple of metres and embraced him. It was a gesture of a great force which inevitably carried me away. Here I see myself a brief moment aiming at Dioniris' body, then missing it, then I no longer see myself for I leap, I have taken aim at him, I am catapulted I brush against him I don't touch him I miss him: he is effaced, he has stepped aside he has pushed me back he abandons me where love is where the bond is where reality is, all the dark water of the high sea would not lessen the shame which burns me.

I fall, I fall laughing.

He picked me up. I stare at him from top to toe through a bar of tears. What does he know? I need him I need him, I must bathe in his laughter plunge into his living flesh without being afraid of tearing it, but I barely dare touch him for there is the Other and him whom I do not know who moves who is now here now here as a third

When he describes the Other to me he compares her to a snake with several mouths to his heart turned against him to a Mexican sacrifice in which he would be the priest the heart the wrenching of the heart the knife and his teeth and above the cavity, he-Dioniris, shining, horrible, the sun, says to me that what makes the Other formidable is not destruction and pain, it is that he is himself the bond of this evil that the flesh which loves is also the flesh turned against us, that if he weakens or becomes distracted the Other attempts to supplant him or sometimes to seduce him.

We shall never be alone any more. In those days I became Three, and he too was never alone and felt like Three. We were the necessary couple, two dancers face to face slow and fascinating and two knives between their teeth. We made love not far from death, right on his bed. We were able to live to the letter in the presence set with his disappearance, split by an exhausting knowledge, we were alive and immortal like our books, ready for the definitive inscription in the library among the sacred texts we the only secret text of the Other as a third, unforgettable for any memory, among the delusions and the shrouds the living veils and the dead veils, forcefully proceeding with our paradoxical readings playing Love against testaments and Desire against the arrested things the frozen waters and the bed of death in an unlivable re-emergence of all knowledge. How to tell on a stiffened notebook of the intense agitation of our bodies amid this bed of an inconceivable war in

which what killed and what was killed mingled a
shadow with our shadows where we were doubled
spied upon preserved anticipated reproduced and put
back into play by our own completion, how to tell of
the bed of absolute contradiction. It cannot be told
without cutting what would be told, it cannot be told
while cutting one must cut.

Thus: it was a bed of most staccato notes, clipped,
incantatory, necessary, to keep him alive afterwards: the
bed of the absolute vulnerability of the unapproachable
enjoyment of the sex without sex, a bed of terror other
than sublimation, other than flight, other than Other.
He was towering imminent and I was able to take it all
in one go, his seed his knowledge and his death, or in
the extreme poverty rejecting me to wander some time
still on this side of our real bodies, on the fringe of an
abstract body without pain without memory and without body. Or: to take all.

Thus: to write knowing that death is in the text.
To write for a reader already buried the body of this
reader. To be the mother who for some time survives
the son, and worse: to be the father of an only son sole
reader and first lost. Thus with our story: forever illegible. A heirless story, deposited in a place where no
reading passes.

We enjoyed the impossible climax of disoriented
beings who no longer know whether what brushes

against them is their joy or their luck the Most Young, the Most Old, the Most Alone who do not distinguish their right from their nakedness their left from their weakness their ordeal from their fate. Who cannot do otherwise than pluck up their deaths at the root of their lives, etymologically.

In those days we made up a Threesome. *He* was able to say: 'You will hate me when I am dead,' at the same time, and I entered in the notebook the sentence which he will not reread. I was able to think: He's going to die, he has his death. It is ours. I take it all. It is in him where his life was. Inevitable. Nobody but us knows, and the Other as a third and always there, the yester eve of our now and always his Lust.

A third of our thoughts forward, a third alive, a third for the grave

Three could be All. I take All

What I do not understand is understood for me. I know how to love him in his life without having it and in his story without living it. I know how to take my desire for our reality. Dioniris' proof is the love which I feel for Him entirely as a third [*tout en tiers*].★

But the very big proof of this love is the unreserved tenderness I feel for his death. I take it all: I want his birth and his ancestry, I want his body born from me, I have an embryo in my hand, I imagine it to be lively and fragile, one can recognize my larva-squirrel, I put it in my heart, I put it in my belly, I go and fetch it where it comes from I swim across full seas and I tread upon evacuated seas, I go back thirty or fifty years not without curiosity, thus I know from which subtle conjunction of laws of coincidences of human work of passions of thoughts of counter-thoughts he is the unique product, and I make an illegal seizure of Him, then I reduce this time to a caress. Then I am not unhappy. I am capable of loving him in the greatest swerves of passion, I feel a sincere tenderness for his death. If he had a bride I could love her if that bride did not leave him I would love her there would be Three of us but nothing would separate me from Dioniris and if that bride had always been there I would adopt her I would feel for her the unwearying tenderness of an adoptive sourmother: nothing can prevent me from getting near him.

What relation between her entirely as a third and us? The non-relation

If my desire has three days in order to build a bed-castle I shall erect a fortified yet beautiful monument in order to know all the radiant outbursts and all the movements of love and all the marvellous contradictions of the loving who know they are mortal: I demand of myself the creation of a vulnerable yet inaccessible house where the mountain effect be expressed to please him and the effect of waters to lull us. At the cost of a considerable amount of work, I wrench from the miserly walls of the Most-great-city the glass plates and the gold joints which I need. Besides this town is no longer interesting: it proceeds by itself to its own demolition. As Dioniris gradually withdraws the highest walls crumble into dust, whereby it is shown that the real is on our side. We witness an immense effacement, a material denial of the place by the self, and while I build above the pocket of waters a glass arch I see the buildings shrink to their symbolic dimension: in reality, severed sections remain erect, extorted from primitive structures and as thin as sheets of paper. In what remains of a most delicate temple a useless tongue still hangs flapping. I erect an arch, mobile, neither bed nor book, small yet sublime, a spherical enclosure sealed by a sliding door and whose terraced roof is gently bulging and transparent; the joints, the only fixed points, are in gold. The pieces are sewn edge to edge with white thread with my hand. The whole is similar to Adonis' cradle, perfumed, floating between the lands: imagine a work of mourning which would seek to combine memory and forgetting and you will be led not far from this provocative simple hall of life, a navebed where the imaginary and the symbolic are wed to each other, where anticipation lies in the memory not far from the Sex of Gold.

There is a kinship between this bed and my notebook and between the bed and death and

between death and us and the Sex of Gold
and the materiality of the bed and of our bodies:

what is woven between these infinitely diverse bonds
through which death, the sex, He and I are the products
of a same desire, through which death may be life and
the son may be wed by the apparents, is a kind of
ungraspable veil except in one paradoxical point,

It is the textamant the one which envelops the Beloved
in the gold linen and lets the Loving One wander outside the linen, very near,

Then I will burst open the linen, alone [*lin, seule*],★ or
with the help of Love which drives the Loving One to
split the veils,

And I will contain it in the text of me,

Why was the veil important for Dioniris, why did I
never manage to put on the transparent blouse which
he had chosen for me without getting hopelessly tangled in the cords which hemmed the neckline so well
that in the end I left it to his fingers, and he tied and
untied these braided laces with amused dexterity

Note: There was a boy who had been born with a caul.
Yet his life, ordered in principle by luck, appeared to
him like a riddle: all happened as if the caul had con-
stituted itself as a universal substance after his birth and
blocked his sight, doubtless protecting him against
death but preventing him at the same time from having

152

access to life. This man was neither happy nor unhappy but tormented by extraordinary cravings; he could have been born in reality only in practically unrealizable conditions: he would have had to be his father's son without passing through the mother; and to have a child from his father without being a woman. Because of the difficulties which he encountered in reality his caul was used as a hymen and was torn only when his adored father gave him an enema: when the faeces went through the anus, he could see for a very short time the world with clarity. Strangely enough Freud, who relates this story, states in a footnote that his patient's caul could not represent the hymen, for 'virginity carried no significance for him'.

Tombe could wonder why the hymen carried such significance for Freud.

What inconceivable bond between the life or death of Dioniris, my arrival in Peruvia where I expect nobody and the destiny and the pen

and what is veiled, what bond between the leaves of yester eve, the ripped paper, the pen and our bedsheets, and what bond between the in life and the wild bed

And now you are gone, and now down which way [*par quel chemin*]⋆ to stroll back to you, and on which parchment scroll [*parchemin*]?

I take the notebook on which I shall lay us when History goes back in time. Do you want me and you to make a superb hymen in Peruvia, some time away from History beyond the pleasure principle where below the sea waters the river of Fire flows I shall keep everything and consign *Tombe*?

What bond, impossible to untie, between the anchor and the waters, and between Dioniris and *Tombe*, between time and its eternity

which scroll brings us between death and its perdition

Earth had to return to earth and memory to memory, and Dioniris then to the counterbook. The original is kept or isn't, close to the Sex of Gold where I buried it, in Peruvia. It is a counterbook made up of several heart-rending notebooks illegible without the greatest anxieties. This counterbook exists but it cannot be found even by me. It is possible that through the mysteries of chemistry which govern writing it decomposes while producing its writing indecipherable in human light. *Tombe* is but a faint emanation of the book of books, a remainder, the effect of pain and not pain itself and, in truth the effect of this effect.

> There were Three of us
> and only one Sex of Gold
> He the pen I the anchor [*ancre*]★
> and on the book cover a single gold stain
> We were reading the stories and the living-world was returning with this great impulse of the repressed which passes through Peruvia
> the river of fire and destiny was shooting at us at point-blank range Fire Fire

I fell as slowly as Him on the bed of leaves
And then, no matter death, absence, separation, weak-
ness, the other, in front,
this colossal edifice of the Text from Then On [*d'Ores*]★
and I set about going round the
Out-time [*d'Hors*]★ and in so doing I was ceaselessly
Outside Myself For Him In Front Of Him
I, noting down, He, dictating and reading,
And struggling, and from one and the other body
making the counterbook such as it can be bound to
infinity,
—And the Other altering us—
You can see us still struggling in this book you can see
us standing once again and once again alive tall ample
naked in contact with the earth and the air and the
range of waters and the movement of planets, brushing
aside the veil which hides human societies, you can see
us as a third
Open, and enter:

I can see him still never lying, indescribable, in the regular movement of the walk treading the blanks with
the rigid grace of the one who walks on the watery
floor.

We found it so hard to clothe ourselves sometimes since
it was so necessary to be naked when he was still alive
and we did not have enough skin flesh eyes sense to be
and to have each other we were never naked enough
to see to engrave to keep each other, each aiming to be
loved for the other me for Him and Him for me given

to be seen, so that the clothes were floating some distance away from our bodies (imagine the vessel and above the bare masts sails unfurled docilely suspended down the middle despite all severed rigging)

Enter, and bring the notebook of sails near where the desirable inscribes its effacing path from one blank to the other, and now if you want to see,

keep watch,

and if you can walk on water then move forward and you will see the shimmering face which love turns towards the Other, come near, and if you want to know whom the Other resembles, read the drunken bedbook [*lis l'ivre litvre*],★ trembling and, beneath our tears, liquid, and beneath our bodies still virgin now and still always quite other

And why, I ask myself, the fatal outcome, which for Dioniris presented itself as an untearable, yet transparent veil presented itself to me under the guise of a strict and beautiful woman, unknown, and ageless like the gods which nothing alters, but quaintly human and known and yet ageless and not mortal, always present if we had eyes to see her and therefore issuing from us and yet often absent dissolved and then scattered like the smell of Lovely Mint on the body of the beloved.

We leapt from one moment to the next with uncertainty and precaution disturbances of a moment at a moment disturbing each moment of another passion

Secretly I sorted out, I removed infectious words from our air, all those that brush against death, the end, history and their contraries, life, continuation, resumption, age, all that even remotely caused to throb by chance or contiguity or by sense or nonsense the risk to die making me tremble as if the very trace could contaminate, as if I feared because we were that couple and not one single object at the unlimited angle of time and of the end of time, lest it might introduce its eventuality at the very point where we were joined.

Naively, skilful, tense, unrelenting, I filtered. However, I was not wary of the axis of substitution. There—but I was not unaware of it—my watchfulness frayed and the risk of sudden re-emergence cropped up suddenly, disappearance is inscribed everywhere and appearance does its work and wherever the couple is inscribed its disappearance straddles it. I did not want to exit the game-without-exit but to isolate the part in a provisional eternity.

All that is not us will be us.

We shall write the book which is beyond the book.

The One will not be without the Other.

These laws applied infinitely to whatever wherever our bed was delirious between the gold linen sheets where each one of us bent over the other is returned to us, each makes the shadow of the other and the other simultaneously. 'Write!' says Dioniris, I write or I don't write according to whether I am myself or Him, Dioniris, the one of us who does not write but without whom I would not write and nothing would be written, but it is Him who invents *us* beyond the couple that we make when Love produces us by playing our bodies. There is Him and Me and beyond there is Him-Us and Us-Me and beyond stands Love which envelops us and weaves us and plays Him, Me, Us and all that we risk against death and which takes aim by playing our bodies which, played, produce Love, to straddle death and turn it just as Dioniris cleaves me and I straddle him. Thus in this economy all that is not us will be us, thus, and as long as we make that love, pushing our disappearance from one edge to the other, who would dare approach us and without interruption, this delirium on us and issuing from us makes the wandering-bed for us the one which floats sailless above the pocket of waters, who would dare

(Enters, between all that is not us, without noise without gesture without doubt the semblance of a woman, an apparent non-woman a woman who resembles no woman, identical to herself only, impassive, and yet having appeared slowly before my eyes she resembles.

And yet she does not exist, and yet here she is, altogether other, and before my eyes capable of seeing her she alters

And yet here she is as you can see her in dreams.

And her perfume ... unforgettable. A name can be for-gotten, a face erased but I would recognize this woman's perfume among ten thousand, more bitter than the smell of mint and sourer than myrrh and more intoxicating than cinnamon

Before my eyes she lies down indifferent, non-human, and as I was examining her forcefully she makes herself similar so similar that I must have recognized her then

I said nothing I silenced her

She does not enter she is here,

interrupting us, an unexpected woman on whom He does not even cast a glance. I'm the one who makes the provisional connections with the external world. I take her before my eyes because of a distant effect of likeness for an apparent of Dioniris' or mine. Or a florist or a chambermaid, clad in a red dress and with-out make-up. She puts on a shy air. She makes it clear in a faltering voice that the huge bunch of thick-bundled roses she is carrying in her arms as if it were her child is meant for Dioniris. I can feel his envious strength bribing the air around us, one moment, through a quaintly biting glint which discloses an unexpected, stronger gaze in his clear eyes, it is Himself she resembles. She adds that these roses are not made to be kept but thrown, under his feet, on his bosom, on his thighs.

Slowly impassive and similar one thunder-striking moment in every single feature to Dioniris altogether other

I gave a start He three times more handsome than Himself

Naked with his back turned never like now ripe for death with blusher on his cheeks a mere immortal

I got frightened I said nothing

And now I still have not said anything)

From where we are if in play we so much as open the curtain we can see death dying from being death and the placeless bed wandering veilless on the other side

(It's to me she spoke it's I who recognized her I saw her suddenly resembling Him, it's I who got frightened)

Yet still held back and keeping in the inviolable vicinity of the Sex of Gold, with bent face, receiving still directly all the marks which Dioniris was addressing me, or almost

All . . .?

(Yet it's I who recognized her I sensed the bond which attaches Dioniris to the unknown woman but I said nothing.) Before my eyes the apparent becomes restless and gloomy. She asks me in an almost inaudible whisper 'Are you one of those women who . . .' I reassure her straightaway, with protective swiftness and even with amused gentleness, No, no, I am not one of those women and we are not like those who ... her fear reassures me, why would I fear the one who fears me? I also tell her to placate her that I am not a young girl either, nor a bride, nor a virgin, I am the concubine, and no there's no other law here than ours. I cut off the discussion here. Let her go.

Naked with his back turned never like now ripe for death deaf blind absent to all that is not us

Let this remain outside and annul itself, let him know nothing let the oh-so-fragrant roses dispel the smell

Silenced the apparent lessens

Which obscure bonds between the apparent and desire and us naked our body united to another light

Let Dioniris not know it

Before my burning eyes she darkens, she writhes she dispels. I can still see her smiling faintly.

He, such is his force of concentration, his nakedness, his mastery that he lets nothing show: he is not there, but white and reserved almost absolute, always virgin, the Unapproached without relation to the Other in relation with the Other on the mode of the non-relation and I gave a start, He Dioniris intact and always identical to himself immortally calm.

(It's I immortal being who saw her with my eyes, my fear recognized her, I flinched)

Now she effaces herself now she returns, dark and crimson, the one from the outside who wants to attract us now she looks at us and she resembles us

I close my eyes and I cut

But no sooner have I opened my eyes to see him again than his envious strength throws her athwart and my desire falls back topsy-turvy and doubt and corruption here's my fate

She returns. What does she want, that one? To return. I no longer need to turn back for she settles unceremoniously where we are at an angle with our own shadow ... and I recognize her perfume.

At that moment my back was bent, my legs folded between the folded legs of Dioniris lying on our bed, and I took down in hasty jottings scattered on the bed-sheet and on my skin what Dioniris was dictating to me bodily ('Take, take, take,' said the voice) on the body and in us and I took without taking the time to reflect and where I could, for it was the textamant, the text of texts, which was to help me make our bed again on another bed, when the latter was overtaken, when our elements are scattered outside any known time, and when the senses are separated from things and ties untied and the weight is isolated from objects

and when the absolute sex is without place, without land or sea, and separated from its sperm,
I took everything in haste and where I could receive it, with cut-off, broken, yet persistent jottings

even on my very cheeks and neck, and on my breasts
and my belly, and the tears of his myrrh
But overrun or fearing to be so by this panspermia
Leaving chance its share and fortune its share and the
Other its null share anywhere

She returns, she who wishes to be known more
and more red and envious, and takes position under his
still virgin eyes

And I have not opened my now useless mouth,

The curtain raised, which curtain? which bedsheets
or eyelids? after years of effort, the riddle remains
unsolved for me: Whence is it that one minute *too early*
I saw her, the craftswoman forbidden to the eyes of any
living being? I should have erased her, but I managed
to do so only in part, this constantly forced me to bear
right, so that the right half of my body half turned away
from us through this effort was heavy and distorted this
supreme moment. Or I should have resorted to Him,
but I would have plucked my tongue out rather than
interrupt him then, and it was my business, had I not
received her, reassured her, rescued her. Or (invent the
curtain which does not rise) I should have driven her
away I don't know why I hadn't done so, or else it was
because of the resemblance she displayed with either,
this woman did not move, and I put up with her, pre-
ferring to steel myself than lose the sight of Dioniris
for one hundredth of a second. It was not a woman and

I was not fooled by roses. The desire which rose from her stank me out. She wants someone, that one, how could I be mistaken? I must have seen her getting ready, piling up. Where were my eyes looking were they these eyes, my eyes were in Dioniris but all that exists is reflected in Dioniris, I could not understand why I had not understood, was she absolutely unexpected or else was it the unexpected which I should have expected, but I alone, precisely, because she could not have been unexpected nor expected by Dioniris and that her visit, contrary to what I had believed, was meant for me personally. This woman was bursting with envy. Is she real or unreal or?

He, reflecting us and his sex only, blindly or not, pointed at me, oriented towards my bent face, was speaking to me gently and attentively:

'Take, and you will recognize us by the smell and taste. You will trust your mouth which does not see, your tongue which does not hear, your nose which knows my present body, Take, and when I am dead do not kill me, You, be faithful and keep me alive in you.'

As for me in this moment which was side by side with absence, my heart fails me still now I could not swallow, I was not able to, my tongue did not taste, my lips did not keep, my throat remained virgin, I did not eat, I did not drink, I did not keep him when his sperm was still alive, I pressed my lips against his root and I let these most precious tears flow down my cheeks and my neck, in this inexplicable moment Love betrays me and turns away from me, and no sooner had I let these precious notes be lost than I felt myself pierced beforehand and for ever by the fear and hatred of myself, And now the source of the sperm has dried up. What is lost is irreplaceable, living things can no longer go through me, and my throat aches through which life did not pass, without this ache hurting me even—all that senses and desires and all that lives steers clear of my senses nowadays still—I hear, I see, I breathe and I have lost this body for which I should have given my life, I remember it but it gives itself to be seen heard and tasted a little beside my senses.

He who knew everything, said nothing, but his eyes wandered over my infernal face with the very gentle tired distant yet soothing gaze of a forgotten Semifather.

I could use as a pretext the presence of a third party, invoke, without lying, that the demon of modesty, because of the apparent, did me this wrong, but I could not delude myself. Nothing could separate us, except myself. I did not drink, I did not know, I spat out.

Then an extraordinarily violent scene occurs, a killing without any apparent trace, but which revives in the darkest depths with the blood poured out by the unbridled heart the most forgotten and infantile demons, this kind of epigraph of a delightful cruelty which cuts any biography short and relieves you of your power and reason and holds you back by a snapping thread on the verge of existence and forces you if you still wish to live to connect the uninterrupted fragile thread to a foreign line which animates you and reweaves you into quite another story than the one you were producing and which has carried you till here where the economy of passions and the production of personal time happen in a way which would have seemed to you hateful before the break-up and which seems hateful, even intolerable, to you after the fact and which however is yours which you could not possibly reject without disappearing, so that you cherish the intolerable because it is now the only trace of your previous nature and you are at the intolerable point of your story where you are also what you are not where you cannot be what you are without desiring at the same time your liquidation where you no longer know whether you are other than an invention of your hatred where something in you remembers or boasts of quite another story. And when you rip your bedsheets apart in the morning in the struggle which opposes the two natures which lie in wait for you when you wake up and you know beforehand and again which one will prevail, you attempt to flee bewildered you hurl yourself brutally onto the wall thinking you've found the door and your right is your left and you wander between two subjects which you are not and which repel you fleeing between two mirror partitions which shoot at you which spit at you which make fun of your despair and return to you the mismatched pieces of a being in which you cannot remain fleeing between two walls too close together for you to be able to slide along unscathed and which, with the memory outside which you attempt to stay and the forgetting which remains barred from you, make up the grindstone where the unhappy who are dispossessed of Self throw themselves of their own accord. The head considers the body to which it is riveted with loathing and turns away from each of its gestures, the uninterested rudderless lawless body reverts to savagery, the present is a bad eternal dream the real is a bad eternal-present and you are suspended at the angle made by what you no longer are with the shadow of what you are outside the scene which was used as an epigraph to this infernal work which is being made without you but which you triggered off and which decomposes you, and you are lying on the border as if dead yet without enjoying the benefits of death, mocked, knocked over, deformed, and you throw up, it is this vomit from now on your life which you bring up, and you wipe your lips with the curtain.

This scene did not last more than three minutes, maybe three seconds only, and it did not take destiny more than three seconds to undo the work of so many years, and to deprive you of the inheritance of generations, of acquired wisdom of your goods your habits frames and categories, of your chains and alliances, of your growth plan, all this immense edifice collapsed in one stroke but the loss is nothing, what is unbearable is what was substituted in one stroke for your system and which gives you the frightening feeling that this stroke had long been prepared, nurtured by someone very close who knew your secrets as well as yourself and was waiting for the first opportunity to despoil you, thus to the anxiety of loss is added the anxiety of exchange and to the anxiety of exchange is added the harrowing certainty that there is somewhere in the world a person very close to you, close enough to understand you and know you and who wishes you ill not wishing you dead but wanting your life your very substance, and to this supreme anxiety is mixed what allows you to survive outside memory outside yourself, out of sight, the certainty that what you have lost endures somewhere at least in a vestigial state, and even that this inimical person is somehow at once repulsive and reassuring, allied or related, by marriage, inheritance or subversion, or jealous identification, and you do not deny this bond through which went the act of the other blood which degenerates you. There is a hole in the body through which anything can go in or out which must be spotted and, if possible, closed.

If I had drunk and made mine the substance I spat out I might have avoided the inevitable, I would not have been diminished but if I did not drink maybe it is because I was already diminished, would I have swallowed if the apparent woman had not been there, if Dioniris had not been close to death would the scene have found place, if the sheet in which I wiped my lips secretly had not already threatened me with mourning, these questions make the story of break-ups which throw me into another story so that when I am in a bed I also dream in another bed and simultaneously I am dreamt in another bed besides and I am acted active and acting through my simultaneous ages,

I could feel the breath of this woman on my shoulder, she was leaning over me who was leaning over Dioniris. Suddenly she made a familiar gesture which persuaded me at once to change all that, which I would have done with a great fuss if I had not been afraid of disturbing Dioniris. Three minutes or three seconds later, all was changed, I was lost. This woman, the apparent, had first had, while leaning over me, a libidinous look which would have enlightened anybody more blind than me. I should have chased her away then but rather than interrupt Dioniris I resigned myself to putting up with her provisionally even if it meant expelling her with yet more rage a little later. Then she made this familiar, humiliating and, I felt it through my skin, envious gesture: she caressed my back with a hand trembling with a desire to strike, besides throbbing only for Dioniris whom she was aiming at through me. I should have straightened up then or warned Dioniris but I hated the idea of turning him away from us and I hated

myself for giving in to a third party and did not want to
make this intrusion worse. I was driven by a sort of protective instinct which I would not have had normally
but which was dictated to me by the strange state of
Dioniris who seemed to have withdrawn from any body
in order to concentrate his presence in his voice and in
his sex so that his eyes were open and bright but dazzled
and sightless. I was afraid, I covered him with my body.
At the moment when the hand of this entirely third
woman had touched me harshly, I understood the worrying nature of the bond which united her to us, I also
discerned, but with less certainty, the origin of these
alterations which gave her the semblance now of Him,
now of me, I also knew what unenviable role she played
in our Love, but also in certain respects what enviable
role and why she could not caress me without hurting
and frightening me; besides the poor woman had the
face I saw her with, according to what I thought or
expected from her and this body of a mature woman in
mourning and this threatening libido could belong only
to the one who had always wanted to take him away
from me since the beginning and whose enterprise had
marked Dioniris' entire flesh as early as his birth or
before. I detested her, I dedicated to her my most war-
like thoughts when I heard her speak without even low-
ering her voice. She insulted me, she threw back at me
loudly the reproaches which I directed at her in silence,
she accused me of theft of murder of treason; she spoke
to me in a foreign language either for Dioniris not to

understand or to create between her and me a sly complicity she repeated three times ten times three times
the same sentence, the only one in this speech which
hit me powerfully: I did not want him to hear, I was
beside myself with worry, if she insisted, if she translated,
if she prevailed, I could see Dioniris following this scene
without taking a part in it, neither an actor nor a spec-
tator but with the strange calm of a reader who knows
that what is written does not bite, without moving
without covering himself without intervening. All this
lasts one minute which still lasts where I am, a sharp
minute, that when this whole story since our origins
changes sides and separates the one who did not write
from the mean dubious yet submissive and, even so,
faithful secretary whom I became.

One minute later he would no longer say 'take' to
me, he would say 'remember', one minute too early the
veil ripped apart

I turn against the apparent, and I threaten her and
beg her. Let her go away, let her allow us to live these
last days in life, let her not be recognized, let her not
assert her rights. I speak in a very low voice, in a hasty
murmur I tell her that if Dioniris hears he will suffer a
lot more, that if she steps aside I shall not attempt soon
to hold him back, that if she imposes herself I shall resist
on the contrary with the help of all the divine human
magical ruses at his request, I demean myself, I promise
just anything yes yes without thinking driven only by

urgency. She goes out saying she is waiting for us outside. If I had been able to kill her, but precisely it was
impossible to kill her. I look down I cut.

No sooner have I closed my eyes than Dioniris says:

    And what happened that I could not see?
    What did she want? Dioniris, real alive, asks me.
    To hear from you, to hear from us
    What were you saying?
    You were afraid of her.
    It was a friend of my mother's, I was astonished, I
    did not expect her, I told her I will see her later.
    Later when?
    Another time, elsewhere.
    Why do you speak elsewhere
    another time to another than me
    I am not your son why do you stand in front of me
    My desire moves away from you why did you drive
    it away
    You behaved with me as if in front of a departed
    Why did you suppress me
    I speak I am here my presence is real and alive I give
    I remain
    You spoke in front of me as if in front of a man
    deprived
    Of life, of sex, of strength, of intelligence, of pres-
    ence
    Where you are you make me disappear already dis-
    appeared

Listen, I speak here, I hear here,
And I still know I have always known the Other's
language
I read what you think, I heard what you said
Why have you already forgotten me have I not
remained among real things.
You cover me with your body, have I asked you to
cover me
You will cover me when I am dead
Why do you drive my presence away from your
presence
You covered me with words
Why do you want to enjoy my death before my
time have I told you I desire him and do you wish
to bury me
Have I not stayed for you do you think that I have
not already postponed a hundred times I could
have delivered the envelope to you a hundred times
and broken the suspense but then I hedged a hundred times and without saying so have I not given
you the absolute present
You have not known me
Your love falls on me from a place where I cannot
be and kills me
And what has happened of what I have not been
able to see?
I had warned you with a divine insistence
Why did you persist?
I had never asked you this kind of question

Tell me first all that has happened
You have to clean up my imagination
Do you imagine what this woman may be
What news of this woman
For things to happen thus you had to work at it,
didn't you?
Who speaks to you behind me
Say the name.
This woman was calling for an answer
Give me some news first
How come this is renewed?
Before you speak I tell you hear me
You know me
Am I not true to my word
I had warned you with a divine insistence
Your breath takes my breath and effaces it
You love the one I would have been when I have
ceased being
There are three of us our name in your heart is
Three
You do not know me alive, you have spoken in
front of me as if I were more-than-mortal and I
have heard everything
You bought me you sold me
You gave me the lie, me full presence, you the trap
Me the real you the unreal
Why do you want me to be more-than-mortal,
If I was immortal would you love me and if now I
no longer left and if I stay?

You know me a little
I've told you all.

All, then, was said, all here was done. Nothing
could happen to me any longer, nothing can happen
to me any longer than what happens to me from
Dioniris and all had happened,

Who can do so that what has already happened has
not happened, that one would be Dioniris, but that one
is the one who will never happen, only that one could
dictate the other story the one which can undo what
is done, turn time upside down, that one would be
Dioniris,

And now now I can I dash forward I cannot now too
late

Is it me who wants what I want yes no and then
here where to want did I want what I didn't want or is
it deliberately wanted and so on do I want, what is
deliberately wanted, etc., but I don't want myself it is
me who does not want myself no I don't want that no
yes, etc.,

nothing comes out of my throat I am deprived of
screams

He, Dioniris spoke for a long time, he lived, I could
hear him, I adored him but my flesh had lost all the
privileges of the real and I could not reach or receive
my eyes burnt beneath my forehead

It's Him over there, impassive, an excessive metre away
from me all separates us nothing separates us except all

I could reach him but I cannot the present separates us for I am in the grave of my body and all that happens to me is past and I steered clear of his non-mortality and I fell into the memory which carts the bodies of dubious lovers along, all that ties one to the other was cut off, the whole canvas of us split in an inhuman realization of the detachment which had occurred when I had allowed favoured accepted desired the ambiguity of the veil, cut the shroud right off the sheet of hymen, made peace with the woman in mourning, subtracted presence from the present, supposed what has not happened to have happened, forced pierced the real out of cowardice. Cowardice now makes fun of me and tangles me up, only He remains clear the whole inaccessible and yet so close that if I had the right the courage the strength to touch him really it would be possible but I am prevented I am beside Him but he is impregnable

I am swimming far from here between two thousand rocks and there are no waters, my flesh gets torn on the stone crags and releases me, I am torn into a thousand pieces but the pain is not returned to me and I do not weep.

What I am is where I am not. I see Dioniris, I hear him, when have I touched him that was three thousand years ago we were making love in a merry, juvenile, bright and doubtless bed, huddled closely together in a superb magnetization of all our possible ages and without thinking. I remember.

'Remember,' says Dioniris and it seemed to me that each unforgettable word moved me away a thousand years still without my body, neglected by me, having made a movement; if I was the word on his lips oh if I was the next breath and if He breathed me out, I would perhaps feel this desired body move but each unforgettable word repels me and fortifies my impotence. His voice pushes me aside, I am not standing in his way. But when I was in his way what have I done have I not recognized from his shadow the right to represent him. His voice is heavy and slow it reaches me after getting worn out against the hard-wearing walls of the years, it is colourless, it is a crushing, broken, crumbly yet incantatory and sad voice. It does not call it does not arouse it drops. Sad, gentle and threatening subtracting me from its presence through the inflection of terrible caresses, then,

too late now

I,

In the place of the dispersed, useless and actually mortal body, a set of bound leaves

and where the happy eyes might have been, in their place, this blank in order to hold back what will spring from him

Will be this notebook which will deceive nobody but me, me the page without Him, indistinct and void, Him the ink for drinking,

Will be this blind face but for Him transfigured, subjected, the only possible desirable being, to the decision of what He dictates to me,

What was once body, dismissed, useless, put down anywhere, putrescible,

i,

Separated from Him and Me and also from Us anywhere I am ready for the Book. What will be written is not written yet

Then later,

If I could read this book where it is Him who is inscribed from one edge to the other, if turning round I manage to reflect myself perhaps through an incredible return of my senses I shall see myself drawing near Him perhaps seized taken over,

Adopted

By The One definitely young hoped for and lost, greater and greater and expected who is the real author of the unwritten book of which this book is nothing but a mourning effect.

'Remember, bury me, keep me, and in the future look for me.'

His face now deploys the complexion of disappearance, which copies the colour of life in order to seduce and makes up with a crimson powder the shadow which does not deceive. His cheeks tan and glow uniformly, his limbs cover in a gold sweat, thus does my Most Precious move away from me and immunize himself. This god whom he becomes, I will celebrate in his name, he frightens me, he is more unique, more naked more forbidden than ever more beautiful too, three times more beautiful than Life, the Unkillable,

The one who does not write but gives himself to be written, the irreplaceable who gives himself to be replaced through whom I, a monument undone by pain and redone by desire, a living tomb an unassuaged notebook, am active,

Interminal, withheld destiny, similar to the too free

sentence reeled off by a syntax powerless to steer its course here or there and so on to the point of delirium

if its comma at last does not step in

—

,

but I was afraid: of what, after the comma, would come about

: of the comma, of the pause, of the order of meaning

: of the weakness of the comma if through mechanical force the sentence happened to carry it away and submerge it, of the force of the comma if it slowed down the movement until in suspense the present enters reality and this wandering bed, be reconstituted,

From this fear I cause a sea to flow [*couler*]★ in which I swim without getting torn without looking for or fearing the bottom without being afraid of sinking [*couler*] which I use as a bed night cloth and movement

I cleave it and yet it is unalterable and natural I drink it without exhausting it, it is bitter salty without opaque excess and pearly as tears of frankincense, its smell: the smell of Lovely Mint, the one that knows that in order to make the Beloved return it must separate him from the new bride.

Dissolved or forgotten or fictitious, the apparent in mourning? (who was waiting outside) (vulgar and impressive like the knocking at the gate of Macbeth's castle like all that waits before the gate, like the gate, the porter, the framework, the rite, the pulse of life against possessive evil, and all that shakes the power of the parenthesis), no matter the mask, woman, other, bride, the envious, with regard to the produced effect, had it been nothing but the reflection of what was committed on this bed from Him to me. All that was beyond me and fell back around us, the very excess of passion and sperm, demanded this detour, I believe. This additional something on the side where to pour the overspill of anxiety which Love then partly dedicated to war could not consummate. Something other which would wait outside, which neither He nor I saw entering through this door designated afterwards. Pre-existent then the one who usually does not let herself be known, the oldest bride, the fateful mother, the one who has always waited outside, if he had heard her he would be dead; unclear, I gave her a hearing. I felt a vague excitement at the very thing which caused me such vivid loathing and without lacking scent, at this smell, at this wild appetite. The curtain raised one minute too early, what does one see? Which obscure primordial antecedents concerning no living person? As the old sisters do not enter, are there, they rush *from close* whisper the fate which onstage plays Macbeth 'off-stage' she, the bizarre apparent who rushed from so close that she resembled me or resembled Dioniris, had always been there, outside tacit evasive lively through the supreme circuit reinscribing the fate of our bed with a brutal finger. We on our stage, she on something else than a stage, at the fold which our bed made with our shadow, outside but not outdoors. I did not see her again, however. For some time I was subtracted nerve by nerve from myself deprived of meaning, in the vacancy of darkness, I an empty place yet still a place in this mortal state of negative proximity which was the symmetrical reverse of the passionate movements which Love used to suggest to me

very / close / extremely / struck / by extreme / separation / separated / yet / within / His / reach / this / forbidden / body / a / short / while / ago / still / mine /, dispossessed of separation, dispossessed of the evil which right to the marrows possesses me, nerve by nerve detached from my bones and deprived of this detachment, any impulse turned against my heart assigned to the irreversible, lost and without hope of losing me annihilated without hope of disappearing, I could hear Dioniris' sad voice and each word from the adored lips, sadder and calmer was the voice more violent the poison of meaning, my blood was fleeing from the detested walls of my veins, my eyes rolled upwards pictured to themselves the One who anticipated-all-my-desires standing and colossal blocking the future by flourishing his dead body, thus outside the place of me abandoned by myself: I could not even feel the pains which had beset me any longer, I was rotting near the one for whom I wanted life

Then rose the very earth through the effect of my severing act: I saw the noble distant surface, which we would not have been able to catch sight of jointly from the wandering bed hanged up by my good offices beyond the reach of matter, rise effortlessly and without breaking and loom up not far from my bones and I saw that she was waiting for me, actively, her black belly was claiming the powder of my bones, aspiring to my pulverization, swelling, getting stiff, tensing her black membrane, the earth itself to my horror had come to fetch me, it was drawing near and demanding me, even of space of the fall and of the crushing I was dispossessed I was the place of vertigo and deprived of dizziness. This canvas separated me from mystery, to crack my skull open on it, to spill my darkness in its night to lead my distraction astray, to travel again in reverse the

vain birth way without going by sea and without leaving any trace, to accept never having been accepted,
and not even to manage to make this desire rise, not to
live not to have lived and not to be known by death,

and held on the edge of the edge, outside the outside
and unacceptable. This tight swollen black canvas,—
with what black milk can this breast poison me, I will
suck it, I will chew it

At last

I will feel the bond which darkness forms with the one
who rapes it: it exposes, in a somewhat fortuitous relation in order to multiply anxiety, the very thing which
seemed to have to remain hidden, such that it is tied
from behind and actually invisibly and what the tear in
the canvas exposes prematurely is the canvas and what
seems behind is what is before

At last I will take the native road. The darkness, not the
night, for it turns out in fact that the whole space is full
of congealed black air. Nothing pierces this negative
light without thickness, but absolutely occult and with
an anxiety at once poignant and exalted I move forward I swim guided by an instinct which knowing it
was madness I decided to trust in the absence of any
clue, light or help, I steer the swimming down ways
which my body reinvents, in unguaranteed connivance
with the perhaps fake traces of sensations of yore: without seeing I move forward with eyes open and useless

led in this fantastic situation without hesitation as if the danger were not external but internal this way that way this way finding assistance only in my recklessness on the other side of fear where it laughs and laughs itself. The excess of fright is then beneficial. I enjoy the exceptional quality of this darkness which opens infinitely on to darkness. I dash towards these cliffs famous for their fierce breaks and their erosion which can be found I don't know where before on this road, I swim

... to tumble off a cliff, to see tumbling, one shouts, or, with blood to the head, one sinks, in the ecstatic instant, or to see tumbling from the foot or from the edge; or to see oneself tumbling inwardly, but passing simultaneously beside the good fall, by dint of having coveted it, crashing down from the derisory top of its small height, once lost the liberating use of real space. Thus towards the real or imaginary but magnetic cliffs, overhung, adopting adoptive fate, moving obscurely yet hastily, I will soon find what is waiting for me now, which, delighted, fulfilling this dream I have of Him during the race: 'He is waiting for me, in the future before which he has taken up position with a raised knife. / I / want / this / gold / knife.'

  Thus, such as is read invisibly:

where that which seems to have to remain hidden is exposed by such and such a marvellous language in which in a worrying detachment of meaning the word is suffixed by its absence where what is said says that it is not where the shout runs along the teeth without getting out of the mouth, where the invisible is unmistakably the only high point only conceivable if not knowable present and torturing present of proximity. Reads to whomever tolerates that it be pronounced which is readable in the dark only, in the given-withdrawn where the gold knife intermittently points towards the Invisible which seems to have to remain hidden, I am hurled wanting what is wanted towards these cliffs which cut or line or qualify the path, knowing it without certainty, preceded, not seeking to go to a designated place but to cross painfully and with exhilaration this accumulation of darkness without imagining what would follow

Over there the knife is one body with the one who raises it and with the cut, and I want it all,

In the dark where all brushes against me incites me and reminds me of my fragility fear is weak and covered up by the inarticulate yet most powerful song of darkness I am called I want to answer I'm coming I'm coming O Most Far insist Call me make yourself heard make me run and suspend your voice

Move back and make the knife glint, it's You!

It's Him the one who makes-me-dive into-the-canvas-of-nights Most Far farthest and I am expected, O You Most Disappointing Most Early, move back and make me come forthwith,

But first the knife and first the story in the darkness of time its quick and too slow unfurling and first the painted curtain

From a fixed sea studded with panting sails representing among its silk folds some disappointing voyage behind which receding cliff plays itself out in the absence of its subject this mine gaping Fate where I miss myself and signal to myself foraging through the folds for the one who yields, flee furious through the gap as I have groped the gathers of the old blouse which only Dioniris' fingers knew how to unlace,

And You! towards whom I rush from so close, Flee, flee

Make me run take me by the eyes and disappoint me

As long as I do not reach I live I come I come I come and

You,

Raise this knife, show it, make it glint, but You, don't show yourself

Move back and say nothing, but sing, sing or make this silence sing

And this darkness and *make me sing* where it sings-of-you, Orphean [*Orphélin*],★ O You, I don't know you I have not held you back I am not done losing you, towards whom I rush

As long as I do not see all lives all is kept alive invisible

If all was seen and visible I would not be mortal, if each one knew the other and the other each one there would be neither night nor memory nor movement nor journey nor bed, but nobody would speak, there would be the absolute sun without any other shadow than silence and there would be no marriage or birth or knots or unknotting, no representation or rest or curtain everything would be exposed

but nobody would have eyes and all would be burst open from time immemorial:

Without eyelids, no eyes:

This is why what seems to have to remain hidden must remain hidden behind the canvas but those who by accident or chance have disturbed that which is tied from behind to the invisible, those see death one minute too early, but they cannot be dead and they are reflected onto the canvas. (The same goes for the one who keeps his eyes open while a murder is being committed or between two births, for the one who can the impossible is not mortal and the one who is not mortal does not love).

If the canvas faded I would see all that will never happen because of which what will happen happens without which what happens would not happen which, if that occurred, would dispel my memory at a stroke, and the succession of times would mistake my dreams for reality and the one would be without the other. Then I would want all that I do not want and would not flee what I flee; the earth would be before me flat and motionless, nothing would prevent me from returning to it without risk and radically and without losing my strength or my intelligence or my height, I would not have to dive beneath the seas in order to reach its bosom or to swim in ponds too deep or too shallow, nothing would divert my impulses from their real object any longer, and time would cease trembling and making me tremble. I would know why I loved Dioniris no matter what and why I loved him in the extreme, and through his life and mine, why I had woven then pierced the unweavable fabric of our two lives and why I had loved him till the proximity of his death and in that which tied him from behind to dis-appearance, and why I had fled:

I remember: a little before the separation I asked him:

'Who are you who make me shiver and flee and rush from my hiddenmost self and who make me write?' He had told me: 'If you knew it you would not write, you would not fear, you would not love me. However, when I am dead you will detest me, and you wish me dead, and for the same reason you do not, and you will detest me.' Therefore I remained and did not run away and I presented my face towards him while making it up, and the veil which I covered myself with hid from me this adored face which I feared hating and hid to Dioniris' eyes what could be read on my features and which I repudiated, I drove him away from me without moving away from him, as befits her who adores a god or one similar to gods.

If I detested him who would I be? I am not without Him, without Him I am not myself, all this is
obscure but I want everything, I want the cut and what
is cut plus the place of the cutting and its edges, I likewise want the empty notebook, the full notebook and
the exergue, the notes of the textamant and the discor-
dance of all the questions. If I detested him would the
canvas vanish into thin air, would I not know then
whom I hate in reality, would not the canvas while
being resorbed carry away the bonds which separate in
order to attach. Then *one must know that all that is nothing*, and if by charm or recurrence Love deposited some
mark then all that which yet is nothing would produce,
through the very thing which binds what is nothing to
what I am and in the space barely as thick as a sheet of
paper, offstage, an extraordinary birth. Something then
would write itself, I don't know what, some prodigious
sentence or still unread text, some story without limit
and without fear. Perhaps I would see myself loving the
Most Near without Love compelling me to flee from
him. If the canvas yielded, which at the slightest breath
makes time stir, prematurely, then I would close my
eyes, I would make another sheet for us out of my eyelids, and if my eyelids faded I would detach my retinas,
I would redo Peruvia and its shadow from the inside, I
would project a thousand sails to be put back on the
necessary seas, and I would keep us alive by inventing
a bed with an irresistible cut: this bed would derive our
desires from its folds, lukewarm as a mother, playful as

a young son and provocative as one pleases it would bring about by its genius the subtlest chains and at last would weave without apparent rigour the couple impregnated by its limit:

one would see, for instance, the celebration of the most astonishing weddings, of a father with his daughter united by his bride, of a son honoured as much as a lover by his mother, of Love with its Disappearance, the incompatibles breaking the incompatible at their foundation in order to show fantastic sudden appearances, and Lovely Mint finding its beloved again.

I would remember Him, Dioniris, with so much insistence that by force or by chance, and through the controlled work of fate, I would persuade him to appear even slightly or to inscribe on a leaf all suffused with the infinite desire of this inscription which perhaps knows only the blank of this desire,

and if perhaps Love aroused him enough, offstage to inscribe, barely perceptible among the incantatory notes, its mark,

A comma of gold, which seeds the text

But when he had said take, take, my mouth had remained dry and I had jotted down hastily on the sheet and on my fear, and no sooner had the tip of my tongue been touched (I would recognize this taste yet I swear among ten thousand) than I had spat out, so that my palate, my throat had remained virgin.

Because of this sickening feint, I fear, if some text could offer itself extra-temporally, lest I have no body capable of welcoming him or no ink living and strong enough to grab him and I am suspended in an interminable mourning for none but He, the Given-withdrawn, could mend the unmendable. This sheet which had absorbed what I had allowed to escape from my lips (and I hid not knowing under the folded corner which covered me whether he could see and without so much as thinking but myself dissolved and spat out and in this minute indelible) still exists, folded, ironed, laid down, kept under lock and key in the chest with the books which had made way for us, and the pen. Except for the indelible piece, cut out by my good offices and which, in my state of destitution, does duty for a place,

by the grace of Love which by desire and contiguity causes to throb all that holds on to its object, worldly or other, by the same slender thread. Nobody but me, (or Him) would feel the weight of this length of cloth barely spread out like a sheet of paper, smooth but made all hollow by his absence, marked with signs with smiles and with caresses, and, in its smallness, greater than the all the seas and lands joined together, infinite yet insufficient suspended, and behind the drapery which I had put up myself, stiff opaque and gloomy, the day when I myself, mad, had made my light disappear.

Alone nobody can do so that what has happened has not already happened. I have spat, I have rejected, I have separated, I inherit, I have archives, I have a note-book, I have a cut sheet of cloth—There's a story—All this is real—There is a direction in the story,—over there; all is withheld—for our defence—it is a tissue of truths. This tissue has one thread only; yet this single thread envelops me, withholds time or threads it, like unwound eternity like a coiled fear like a sadness; this thread makes by itself a funny speech which twines round itself and regrets; for my defence and in order to defend Dioniris. There is a scene which returns, returns and returns: it is the scene of the weird sisters, the old hags who cook up their crime in a tableau pre-existing this one, which would delight Dioniris. They are. Pre-cipitated, already there, yet one minute too many to expose themselves to my eyes. They repeat that what has happened cannot not have happened. They pull at the thread which twines round itself. They say to me that I owe them my life. I thank them. I say that they are good craftswomen; I show gratitude. Then others come, with the same thread, and they say to me that I owe them my life, then an army of craftswomen, of old sisters, gov-ernesses, cousins, apparents, and each flourishes a piece of the same thread says I owe her my life. Until I even-tually get indignant; to whom do I owe my life? At this rate if I am held or if I hold on to the thread of the story, I owe my life to all those who have never thought of taking it away from me, therefore to the human species in its entirety. Am I bound by a debt to all that does not kill me? Or do I owe my life to whoever thinks of giving it to me or withdrawing it from me by knowing me? And I do not live. For The One Only who puts me into life is far from me.

What are you waiting for? Are you waiting? Whom are you waiting for? Who are you who is waiting? the apparents murmur . . . I am without Dioniris. Actually I am not waiting, I live without life, I remember, I bind again [*relie*],★ I regret, I weep in order to wipe my tears, with the piece of sheet which is more precious to me here than Peruvia where no one stands up erect in front of me any longer, I am heavy and limited, a flagstone, an unfinished, posthumous book, I reread [*relis*].★

Once more I Lovely Mint and once more out of bitter constraint and costly affliction I lament, for Dioniris, my pain, has descended beneath the ground of texts.

Even in a dream I do not contradict history: often I meet Dioniris without there being a revolution, without there being an explosion and without there being any movement, for all is just and withheld. I do not even ask him where he comes from I am neither his sourmother nor his bride but something else. I do not tell him I love him. I veil my eyes I veil my lips, I hide all that I am still here where he is not so that no regret troubles him if he could be troubled. I do not ask him if he loves me. I do not describe the pain felt by the loving woman forgotten alive. I am not the right corpse.

Often I meet him the one neither living nor dying who can no longer die. I can scarcely believe it true it's him I catch sight of neither on earth nor anywhere else but inevitably in another place. And now, I know him. A sentence is possible, which I utter in a toneless voice:

'Now Dioniris, I know you.'

He, speaks, to me who would like to make my last bed in his voice very very close to his chest:

'Now, you know me, which way.'

I would like to ask which way? but I do not dare. I do not dare believe either that there is really a definite softness in his gaze for all is changed and it is perhaps merely an illusion produced by my desire, albeit controlled, or by an effect of indifference or strangeness or of death, but I take this softness for what it appears to be, for inevitably I catch sight of it.

'You know,' says Dioniris but I do not grasp the song below the words, and I do not know. But if Dioniris says that I know, if I hide to myself that I know, and if I asked him what I know then I would cast a doubt about his word and I would drive him away. That I know, for now I know him, and I live without life in this fearful space which his absence has hollowed out nowhere for me,

and on the edges, like this blood flower hemmed by mourning

Often it's there that elsewhere I meet him as in a dream from below the Lovely Mint, abandoned, pines for love [*se lamente*]★ and threatens the new bride who tramples it underfoot and kicks it into dust then as in a dream from above it grows again exciting and green from the body of the beloved.

I recognize her straightaway, even though her face is suffused with a gentle mourning. It is the apparent, such as the loss has changed her less wild without violence, her passion spent, either because she has given up or because she has satisfied it, it's her, chaste and domestic

And this is the Textamant.

It is similar to the mature lawful fruit-bearing gentle bride for whom I no longer feel hatred. Through Dioniris we are of the same bed; of the same misfortune, of the same race, of the same trace, if I cross Dioniris' absence I meet her, if I think of him she lines my thought, I haunt her and she haunts me, we are not one without the other, I am her rival where she is my rival, in memory, where I am not she is where I am she may be where I have been she will be where she will be I will have been in a continuation which is exchangeable and reversible, where Three is bound to what divides it through an impossible relation, the one which has not been described yet, I don't know why or else I know why because it can be accomplished only by those, eyeless, who are not afraid of time and age inscribed on their cheeks and no need to write or read, where it can be or has been written, illegible, on the skin of the female or male lover or in the secret body of the male or female lover, by those, boundless, such as Adonis or Dioniris, who flee between the lines, like gods, and who give to read only in white ink and to those among the male heirs or readers who know that the Most Close *is* the Most Far and that Love binds the loving through what separates them, whose eyes see what those who are dead and back here know in the about-turn which strikes them down; and thus write only those whose sperm is eternal or those of the loving women who keep the lively sperm eternal

Here where the non-being can be where the textamant commas itself

Here where He is over there, I meet her. If she was the bride who keeps her I would love her as much as if she were my bride for she is on the same path and under the same crimson arch

And I am the same pain

If I was the second bride who takes him back, she would love me as much as if I were herself or her death for we are kindled by the same fire, and what burns me chars her and what I miss hollows her out and we are face to face in the same tomb.

Sitting on the floor, covered in dark veils, without smiling, without touching any drink, sitting and consumed with the same regret.

Here we are very good there. We are very powerful, the death which preserves us from death is this cloth where Dioniris was flowing between us as from either edge and we either of us together bending over Him, without limit. I make the bed of the whole of humanity, a celestial milk flows through my veins and I am tall as a tower, she makes the bed of all the blessed, and it is the same bed and the same desire; we could in this great identity hold one for the other. A similar mourning kindles us. Because of her pain she is very close to me, my tenderness for her flows where my blood goes, and I love her almost as much as if she were Dioniris. Yet she is a perceptibly older woman than me humid and putrescible her over-ripe flesh moves me deeply, she does not hide the trace of time, she has no eyes for him and I also know that Dioniris was without eyes: if we were ninety years old, she He or I, on a bed of old age, and wizened, and disarmed, nothing would have prevented us from raising the Sex of Gold. She comes, putrescible and noble apparent. How much I love her, the one who has touched Him, how close she is to me! If she was ninety years old I would have towards her the same fiery and adoptive impulse: for I want her, one must find some bond exempt from the rules of generations and perhaps anonymous in order to take give lose and find her again. Then I muse about that which binds what must remain hidden from behind to the invisible and I do that: I sneak behind her, I embrace her, I sit down and take her on my lap, I twine my arms

round her waist, I fill my skin with the abandoned softness of her skin, I smell her, my hands clasped on her
old belly, her perfume known: the smell of fasting, a
mixture of mourning and seduction

to her which no time troubles, almost motionless
and come *from later,*

to her, I show the first page of the new textamant,
she takes it without hesitating, without marvelling at
the envelope and reads passionately, while exclaiming
at least ten times: *Who could have written that?* This question startles me, it is an unexpected text then? Yet this
page has not left me, I have written it, I have folded it,
I have kept it on me, I have warmed it up. What I have
said I do not forget but what is written is carried away
by dreams

*what is written is forgotten in some way, a certain surface
is effaced very quickly.*

But there are sentences which persist, little syntagms which return, return,

A nothing that is

What, in my absence will have been written where
I had written this ancient text besides and inscribed
under Dioniris' dictation? I take the sheet and it is a
letter. I do not remember it any longer. It is my handwriting, I'm the one who wrote it, but indeed I had
forgotten that this first page was a letter, or the semblance of a letter, yes for this letter is addressed to me,

beyond everything

under my handwriting though. Reading her, I am
at once beside myself with astonishment, with embar-
rassment, with joy, with hesitation overturned, dragged
by contrary passions. This letter in my handwriting I
am sure can have one author only. I swear that I could
never have resorted to this language which is word for
word the one used by tumultuous Dionirises. And
could I, alone and sere, have produced this flood,
thrown this young river from my bed deserted by
waters, climbed up those heights which Only Dioniris
alive could jump over

and puts into motion

I too exclaim as I read and reread, I recognized
some of Dioniris' last words followed by others which
are first, and although this letter to me is not signed, it
seems to me that

. . . gone gone all the questions all the filled gaps and
the overturned lacks my hands full of earth are full of
you . . .

all of it

she has read this phantom writing, which my eyes
can no longer get away from, does she know at least,
she must, that I had really forgotten, that a completely
other surface surely got lost which I did not want to
expose, that my reading right now was innocent; that I
did not want that, which my eyes however cannot get

away from, loathe to look away from lest they should
not receive any longer this pang of joy of pain of joy
which does not know itself apart from pain which I
believe is nothing but a delusion but for this delusion
I am willing to disappear from the real and to be myself
as well the apparition of myself, which, deluding, is
more powerful still than what it represents and which
can no longer be since what is written cannot not be
written, and whose effects are very powerful real, living,
striking, petrifying together: no loving woman or
fiancée has watched the sleeping face of the most precious man, uncovered, given over, confident, in more
ardent silence than the silence observed by me whereas
a hundred times my eyes caressed and crossed this
inexhaustible text, and a hundred times the lips of my
eyes or ten thousand kissed in silence the traces of the
unforgettable strength which could have sprung from
one source only. No matter then the discourse of the
verisimilar or the possible, and the whole device which
shakes and wants to uproot or regraft the tree of passions, whereas my eyes allowed only the true language
of the blood to reach me, and what did I care about
the order of the past if the future lived up to my desires.

What has not yet been, who can say for sure that it
will not be? Who can tell what blood or ink which
makes the most burning creatures speak is capable of
giving birth to? Those who do not love to death or who
are not by love elevated, creatures loftier and madder
than what is said about loftiness and folly, how would

they know? they cannot trust their eyes, those who have not seen darkness add to darkness or the day thickening the draperies of the day, to decipher lines to the quick and spasm, the manuscript which had on us, her and me, such a contrary yet also violent effect: me pierced through, in breach of time, at a great distance from myself totally absorbed by this leaf which in its thin space then dragged the surface of the universe with its depths and could envelop the innumerable desires of men and peoples and wind and unwind on both its sides the rich development of history, absorbed in this state adjoining eternity where mourning becomes jubilation, where through an extraordinary stoppage of loss the one who had fallen silent catches his breath,

and the drowned man surfaces on the path of waters. Thus of me not daring to live this time with my body, and only still with my soul and a happiness trembling from knowing its rights: I was reading, examining, looking, seeing, doubting, I do not doubt. If I say to you first thing in the morning: 'Come, a similar sun is born to the sun,' you will chase me away with a confident gesture, and with this gesture of the shoulder, the shrugging of millennia which have led us, you and me, to this morning. Then I will take you to daylight and you will see what was born in the sun and we will agree that you were right to shrug your shoulders then one will have to find another name to the same and daylight will no longer be the same . . .

You will then wait for science to defend its laws
and for an explanation to erase this disorder, but you
will leave me the unexpected radiance. But what is real
or unreal, and what is really unreal?

The other left me, or I did not see her any more:
such was the effect of the violent reading on this couple
which we were a moment before: I, suspended, thrown
into a time which was not a piece of time, but extra-
temporal, some other time, she perhaps into some eve
of a time where she could have withdrawn, for we
could no longer remain face to face before this other
text without either of us being eclipsed. If a proof of
the power of this albeit almost invisible sign was
needed, this movement would be convincing enough,
yet I made no concession to myself, I did not allow
myself to be carried away blindly by some fantasy
sprung from my nostalgia then disguised as reality, nor
by the need to satisfy my taste for the sublime. I was
wary of myself like the plague and I first refused myself
for a long time the soothings of certainty. I behaved in
everything as if the future of my soul were not the issue
and without hearing the complaint of each of the millions of material and immaterial elements of my being
but the calculating and restrained passion of a curious
person on the brink of a discovery. I did not shrink
from the least erotic instruments, I resorted to the aid
of a magnifying glass. I reread twenty times at least and
with a magnifying glass this text with its familiar

mouths. I could also hear it but I refused to be seduced by it, for if I had listened to the song in my veins nothing would have been able to hold in check the intoxicated pack of my hopes and one thousand and one marvellous scenes would already have begot one thousand and one tales ending more sweetly and productively than invented tales.

It was written in my handwriting that:/it was written that—*yes*—, ∞, and there was this sign: ∞, representing the finite held by the open infinite, like the eye held by the eyelids, and the real lined the unreal. This sign was preceded by the word *yes*, underlined by hand, written it seems to me under the dictation of a decisive voice, which could be Dioniris'. I was not sure: the ink was paler at that spot, and that might well have been a mere glitch of the pen, the letters were raised, their angles almost dotted, I was looking at these lines with a magnifying glass, excited by this *laughter* in the text, this symbol which Dioniris used in the past, thinking that I might have reproduced it in spite of myself. I also remember after the fact having thought in the past, when Dioniris had traced it before my eyes, a short while before the age of the textamant, that it was a foreign letter, an incongruous sign, which seemed to me to be drawn from another story onto the bed of ours or to come from a still unexplored language, or who knows, silence this is why this letter outside the alphabet had no name, and in order to say it we were digging with our fingers its invisible nest in the air. If that ∞ now lying there was my work, then I would have committed it in an altered state of consciousness, for never had I imitated Dioniris when he was alive, no more than the fancy would have taken me to imitate his signature. He had told me that this composite sign held for viable contraries, the immortality of lovers, the illusions which could not be discriminated from their hidden objects, the sourmother who knows how to give birth back without dispossessing, and even the Sex of Gold. Where did he get this knowledge from then? I so much dreaded some supernatural, harmful origin which would not have been known to him yet that I had not dared question him. I was listening to him, withdrawn fleeing from and desiring what was looming behind his voice and which he himself could not hear: my body was shaken by the clash of what from very far descended upon us with the white strength of mourning. Was He then warned? If he was without saying so it was because I had to connect my silence to his if he was not it was because I was ranting or I had reached the point where our destinies separated and he was backing away from me with the fascinating movement of the land which glistens as it recedes from the unmoored craft. Down which paper or waterway

Now and now non-mortally you are mine

Between the other and us and now like the vessel blown away by the wind sees the city sinking, thus do

I see the whole of life sinking dark; thus does the day star sink into the ocean bed then

it lays its sagging head, arms itself and with revived gold is ablaze on the morning brow

Yes and ∞ unbound,

On the leaf were lying as a couple and outside syntax, caught in a sentence which was addressed to me and in which a spiteless reproach seemingly cradled itself such that it made my eyelids flutter with shame— (what followed in the sentence on the contrary soothed me and pierced me with hope, as lightning pierces the darkening tissue of rains). This was written:

... what should one do then for doubt to cease ... then in the hollow, lodged without law, after 'the doubt'... *yes* ∞, then, after this couple set in the dough of the text in the fashion of those rings slipped playfully into engagement pancakes and which ostensibly makes holes in the batter, and in the fashion of the first kiss which settled the infernal fate of reading lovers, by putting an unpublished book on the book which another had written in advance and their forbidden lips on rebellious lips, yes and ∞ planted there after 'the doubt' ... like the laughter which fed on this doubt, there was this other sentence beautiful as a wager:... *yes* ∞, what could I do to prevent this doubt' ... I!

here sprang up the Subject of my mourning, the One Alone so much lost which unbound the pieces of my body and forced me to bend my soul. Ah if my life had seen itself forbidden at the end of this sentence I would have gone out of here consoled, borne high by my desire of the One who say I, and by the familiar smell which this question would give off: I thought I could recognize this smell of sea flowers of myrrh of sea rose, which Dioniris' skin used to secrete and which went to my head. Thus the letter's author had replied, however withdrawn he might be below the floor of ages, from this poison which regret distilled from my blood, whose doubt is the product, and which murders the dead and decomposes the most vigorous phantoms. From this invisible margin which continues the margin of the paper to the edge of the Invisible, a voice rose towards me and supported my complaint with its piety. Could I still waver? Did I doubt the One who answered for me? If he had to be believed to be capable of non-mortality, would I fail? Could I not accomplish this effort of the soul for the One who worked at his absence until this prodigious sign of his presence appears? And should I not then obtain a prodigious service from my unemployed senses, hear with my ears this language full of softness which this paper spoke as is spoken by the trunks and branches seduced by poets? Now I heard believing I could hear with my ears what the lips of my eyes repeated with so much softness and my eyes were turning, closing and opening this marvellous text and I felt these two keys closing and opening sentences with so much softness that the air below

this text also reached me and it was indeed Dioniris'
perfume, as if woven into the fibres of the leaf for eternity. It was repeated to me with such sad and wise tenderness and a tone unknown to earthly ears which I
cannot describe, a different tone, keyed to the solemn
and the light, so fluid that it was impossible to disturb
its airs and yet so material that I could be suffused—
the drowned body which death washes up on the sands
beneath the waves, enveloped in waters, the foetus
licked by a tongue of waters, the loving man asleep in
the womb of the loving woman, if they could speak,
they who perceive the imperceptible, water on water
daylight in daylight night around night, would tell of
the harmony of this unheard flowing from the heart of
the unheard—,

If you allow a fragment from the lips, a cell from
the heart, an atom of skin, the germ of an eye, a breath
from the breath, a grain of frankincense, of the One
whom I wanted to be For You, to remain in the universe, this eye will covet you; this skin will caress you
these lips will name you this heart will revive you this
breath will lift you, in reality, and in future, this grain
and after, will make sense for you

Skin silk parchment canvas you can see me there

Already, while I was for one more moment still
doubting my senses, albeit tested methodically and with
severity,—tracing the fateful symbols to the point of
tension, and in all directions, on any substance, wood

paper stone skin canvas silk or ivory, with the right hand and the left hand,—the laughter of the text began causing the numbed system of my nerves to throb and desire returns returns in fits and starts and pricks me with thousands of its minute stings which propagate Love to the most neglected places of the body.

This laughter wets my lips until now still wrinkled like parchment, adorns with tears the lips of my eyes, and now I am all enveloped with this dew, and yet never have I thirsted so much for Him, on an invisible yet most close bed expected for a long time and too long, and in its impatience my heart was tugging fiercely at the natural bonds which held it back within my bosom and my blood rebelled against the immutable circuit which held it back among these sluggish, too-closed limbs, and my desire accused itself of not having already burst open the wall of the tomb and split the canvas of times, in order to stand up at last with red forehead and body stripped from the adornments of mourning and decency in this other native space where I would not fail to find some trace or news from the being who makes me write and weep and swim clear of history.

And now also laugh.

He unmourned carried away by the wind on the sepulchral parchment-like paper

Dry dry I let out a piercing shriek

The myrrh which sees her trunk split by the furious swordfather [*épère*]★ rives asunder with such a shriek, the swordfather while coming down splits it, comes out of it all stumbling,

(and I shed the same tears as the myrrh)

the son three times more handsome and twice son and perfumed

standing moist but safe and dangerous and already desirable with open arms and ready to climax with his soursister another more divine, more scaring birth.

Desire always rushes on to the one twice born twice purloined who is the scarebrother [*effrère*]★ of the semi-father and his fair orphan

And I rushed too, I swooped down on the leaf with the strength of a falcon, it throws itself, ruffled and undressed into space coming down with the strength of myrrh and, in the brief instant of vertigo, it proposes to all the gods the most cruel contracts in order to buy their assistance, it piles up on their plate the pieces wrenched from its body and the eyes hands and sex of the secret loving man in order to make them look away from the dark bed. Thus, panic-stricken, from inferior death to superior death, I break out of the Dioniric chest in order to pick up this paper with no objective value. And now that the son is in her arms the myrrh no longer knows whom she belongs to nor whom she truly loves. I kissed this paper at the corners, on the back, and I was about to place my lips in the middle of the leaf when, sprung out of the much entreated signs, this little thing, an indubitable mobile mark, this curved thorn, this splinter of ink, a semblance of comma, strikes me with its faint lightning: in reality

a tiny little penis, the unexpected child, the sour-mother's scarebrother

Then one can see how the smallest marvellously begets the most great, and the marked text unfurls into context and how through the gentle power of the key which worked within it, this letter has thrown its meaning into our waters

Then before my darkened eyes the text-love is made, the one which I study in the lightless book, laid on my lap in the chest-room all hung with immense sea curtains,

On my left I see the uninterrupted rains falling through the glassless windows and the virile seas which flow onto lands turning red.

On my right through the closed window I see the harmonious intersection of the land of the terrestrial sea and of the lowered sky, and where those three join, at sea level and at the level of human bodies, the big lips of space join in a gigantic smile

And right before my eyes seeded with the small erotic mark the text-love is made in time, felled and sexless

And drenched with exotic tears (just as this drowned boy this friend of Milton's, whose licked disjointed bones cruised the depths of the seas in a monstrous visit, relieved of the ballast of his flesh and thereby pain, but not of desire yet, suddenly emerged, through the graceful force of the friend who knew how to fend off the docile waters in order to keep him) at last

I break at last, in a flood of dreams, the watertight pocket where I was waiting,

Held back to the night to the thousand receding folds by the cord which holds back this cloth on the shoulders and which hope weaves contrarily with despair, at last, I break the pocket of ages, and in a single persing [*persant*]★ cry

I cross the waters from below and the waters from above, so that where the scarebrother is born at the same time as the son and love at the same time as the work of love; and where there is the son the semifather sneaks in, where the comma makes a mark the Sex of Gold is erected.

And I can go back to the sperm's source:

Life of the Comma of gold:

Loud echo of the future text,
Exergue, skyscraper, sole edifice at the extreme end
of civilizations

all buffeted by the strong beats and lulled by the
weak beat, and
from top to bottom monumental and mythical,
Tell again of the fortune of murder to the world:

(Which poet or sage could explain the path of dreams
which leads me now upwards now into the entrails and
cellars of this edifice and binds me through the soul to
the threatening precious chain of those Most-close-to-
death. With their blind Kouroi' smiles, them before me,
towards me, they live and immodestly raise their robes
to show me the Desirable and formidable. Such is the
charm of these strange beings that I no longer know
who I am, and that I want to be nothing more than
what would please them)

Here I am and I see in it [*y voir*], sitting in the
chest-room, at the lightless book, covered in dark veils
without smiling my lips wrinkled like parchment, in
front of the big sea canvases

Very near too far from still ivory [*ivoire*]★ lands and
too near perse airs

Suddenly to pass among the airs above my head the
comma of gold I raise my hand to grasp it by its flame
lock

but its malicious strength throws me backwards

I see it, it throws itself overboard, forcefully towards
the paper bed, lightning quick

I saw again and again the flash of its fall, the trajec-
tory, the tragedy of its decision, the fall, the airs, without

force the tragic force of its decision, throws itself. Bent
... overboard and as if it had lived it all beforehand ...
From either border I bend over I bend over straightaway but right before my eyes the comma crashes on
the paper and its blood spills out. I want it, I wanted it
I've always wanted him that son whom we did not
have. A shower of commas of tears of frankincense
of sons of myrrh comes pouring down now and cries
over me

And makes my mourning its mourning,

And as a vessel carried away by time sees the
inhabited land sinking out of sight so does the whole
of life go under before my eyes and the comma of gold
is carried away below the floor of the text,

I bend over, the rain comes down more heavily,
whitens, raging stormily, and carries me away as Desire
and its commas carry away the lovable remains, no matter how much they went down below the layers of
time, to where the lands rush into the waters of memory, at the angle made by birth with death, where the
comma of gold lives non-mortally,

carried away I swim between two thousand rocks, now
I drawn the sea curtains open now I split the fateful
canvas in order to wrench the future from it, now I turn
over the earth with my hands

Love and its Uncertainties tug at me hither and
thither along the irregular margin which runs alongside
eternity, but what is here and is not over there, what is

not as true here as over there on the coast which bor-
ders eternity,

and now I lift the gold shroud and I wrench yester eve
from the chain of times

How to know what would be how will what will
have been be known if yester eve grows again with the
twice born and if the myrrh puts her semibrother to
time how to know who leads where the comma of
gold falls in what chest does Dioniris with the impassive face vegetate now three times more handsome than
Himself. As in a dream which book would stand up
from a real bed flooded with commas! Thus I muse I
cross I walk along the edge

I know that in order to go back to the sperm's
source one must sometimes go down through the layers
of time, and I go down, yet I do not foresee, I do not
know, I obey the text's injunctions naturally, and by the
fateful signs I am led, I still hold the seeded leaf in my
left hand; thus I go down, but one can say that the tree
goes down and does not rise out of the earth into
which it sinks, and I who go rummaging through attics
or cellars am I not outside time where Love pursues
me without holding me back?

What is not above can always be below, where men
live planted on their heads, their mouths buried, where
others are nailed to the ground by their own penises,
where others come and go and come back with the
frail power of sperm, and I who have known the whole
of Dioniris' body, I am looking for all the remains.

Via down below I go back to the superb source of mourning. He who is afraid of being neither man nor woman, let him hesitate first: then let him follow me till where the margins fade, below the level of civilizations and of their cities, there where absolute parturitions happen, at the Garden of mutations; there where the branch twists back on itself, is impregnated bears fruit and delivers itself naturally

down below where the sons directly come out of the semifather's dreams, and where the very small begets the gigantic, I will be at home: the man who has sown me in the unknown, if I saved a nail paring from him, I will recognize him among others, and I find an eyelash of Dioniris' stuck on my notebook I will derive another Dioniris from it.

via down below where I do not know in which story I have no recollection of torrential and doubtless symbolic rain has swept away the lands and bared the ruins of things and now I see what was buried. Things hold on to one another through strong tangled and arbitrary bonds. Because of that, all is nothing, basically, when waters have taken away the lands and stripped roots. Which bond, still buried or not, between stories and me, between my strength and the strength of rainfalls, between roots and my nerves, between bonds and me? Which bond, except the one which is woven with its contrary, a small tail which cuts the past body which the future will unveil, except almost chance,

what death would be if one were it.

Thus did I muse as I was hurtling down hundreds of steps and crossing the succession of pre-existing rooms which lead to the entrance of the monstrous bottom of the seas, to the sands where are laid those, among the dead, who must not be seen in daylight, longings for children, embryos, mutations, foetuses, the bones of the separated dead lovers whom the shifting layers mix lull and console, not far from Persephony:

Today in the radiance of my running, where I have reached the plenitude of my days, where the richness of my mourning begins to bear fruit, and where my loss is highly rewarded,—I who think this on the left and that on the right, and who lack neither friends nor foes, and who resemble in every single feature and an eye for an eye the sexless mask with which Desire adorns the dreams of separated lovers, I whose patience and loss have cast the body into the mould left by Dioniris in the plenitude of his days

do I desire him and if I desire him who is he, the one whom I can love dead, does the bird-catcher love the bird or the hunt or savagery?

and if one is no longer deprived?

and if I domesticated him if I captured him with a dream, and if in order to keep him then I bedtrayed [*litvrais*]★ him wholly or in part to the other just as the sourmother From above lends the Beloved to the Sourmother From below? Then murder throbs between the one and the other like a terrible alliance and more than once the myrrh's son dies.

So with my desire which my desire cleaves with a terrible stroke as the furious semifather splits the maternal trunk. So with my dream: I dream him alive, from the same dream foaming beasts spring up which set off on our trail, I the flight, I the hunt, I the fury as similar to myself as reality evading its dream and the desired one evading the desire produced by his flight,

I flee, by my side the etymological mothers, as close to my life as to my death, as similar to myself as reality evading its dream,

they in the other story, I outside,

I turn round and . . .!

all has changed I see only the wild boars, then in a now-desolate, prehistoric landscape, I see with terror three wild boars galloping. They run panting like immense dogs, they are the wild boars of the other: I alone have all the fear, I have the fear that knows, I dart into a grave where I go to ground. The beasts gallop like wild horses, they arrive, they come, they are enormous, they separate, two tall beasts hurl themselves in my direction, one disappears eastwards. The two big boars separate, the bigger one, tall as a white horse, with a thick coat, dashes off straight ahead, into the future.

The grave trembles and cracks and I attempt to flee

The big white boar disappears,

The other one, small as a tiger, is a black shining beast with short hair, a real war machine, he charges straight at me. Unpredictable. I do not imagine what he desires, I do not know what he knows, I have to try my luck: if the beast is nothing but brute aimless force, there is a chance I might live, if he aims at me ... In a sort of utmost gamble I do not flee, I face up: the boar draws level with me and brushes past me in a terrifying run, without touching me, ... therefore I desire,

Thus do I muse and immediately I run away from myself as if I were death or the other, just as the bird-catcher runs away from the desired bird I run away from real insane murder by which life attaches me to its contrary,

I cross the world from bottom to top, zigzagging, then I cross the inner cities from one end to the other, then the forgotten battlefields, then I walk along the wall which separates Peruvia from all that is not Peruvia, while avoiding the known or unknown beings, I flee right into the tomb-like depths of the dream.

Just as a flame shoots up from another, so does spring up from my ardour a scene so sad that at this moment and long after tears come much quicker and more ardently to me than words: I reach the arch-basement, where the engines are set up, in the vast poorly lit low-ceilinged hall with no visible far end as is the long unending text of the Vedas. And the heavy piping which supplies the edifice runs level with the forehead which must protect itself.

Leaps up, He! Who but Him impossible there porphyry the air all around him rolled up in the linen of memory is nothing more than the book of his silence

Himself through Himself with Himself hardly visible simple and uncorrupted and almost there

or his perse phantom

But when I see him, seized,

Today if he the Orphan came to take back today the master's post which he held when I had not yet learnt how to read, would he be my master, and could I love him as much as the love I feel for him from here below? would I love him more; would I love him less? or otherwise? now that in the radiance of my running, I have lived, thought, for twenty or thirty years more than him, in this world, and without him, who is he?

I can see in a semi night a bent man, at work, whose slender shape and slim waist, high bowed nape, elegant outline of the ribs beneath the taut skin I would swear are Dioniris' I swear but this cannot be, but through sadness he is Him, and through modesty too and through the nobility in debasement. I reflect the image of his soul no more quickly than he does mine, so that our thoughts form one single silence. We are alike in grief, but mine is turned towards what might have been and his towards what ceased to be: he remembers himself,

'Who feeds (now) neither on fruit, nor herbs, but on the tears of frankincense and on the sap from amo-mum . . .'

The one whom my tears feed is too worn out to bring himself into daylight and produce the external image which could—for a much desired second—resist the brutal action of the sun,

he cannot return,

. . . five centuries of shadow and five ages of mem-ory conceal us and beneath their ashes the nest of unchastity is built . . . where he spreads light cinnamon sticks, here, the sex is more-than-powerful as it is in my dreams and nothing outshines the radiance of sperm

Sadness is born of my joy which immediately stifles it and like a magical plant spreads in my soul the essence which makes one invisible

He-There Dioniris, fundamental and withdrawn, who darns and stops holes, makes a bed of cinnamons and ashes for us, I weave from it the ultimate sheets and the fragrances of the heliotrope which makes lovers invisible/e nardo e mirra son l'ultime fasce.

And: between us, his death, like his secret knowl-edge, and: the child who was not. And between and before us the frail apparitions which his soul wrenches from the scraps of his last ardour, when shaking matter and its laws it undoes with effort the reverse work of Nature, and our images celebrate between two breaths the brief triumphant incests of which the dantexts are born.

But sometimes he turns pale and almost dissolves, and before my heart has found the next beat, shame unfortunately makes up for the effort and reflects it more blurred, with perse forehead, and with feigned body, all trembling, and this tenacious soul blames itself harshly for its intermittence instead of incriminating its Law

. . . all my blood for a sigh from these pallid lips! Let his decomposition fall back on my head and cover it and spikenard and myrrh and heliotrope essence will be our last swaddling clothes. Now each thought of mine hangs heavily over him and exhausts him, and I can see him slowly lifting the heavy plates of air, just as chained absence emptiness and desire weigh down on the limbs of the solitary lover and make him stoop.

He who used to know the subtle clockwork of bodies and make time creak with impotence is now bent over the monstrous body of a typewriter which he is trying to revive. Metal rods, staples, pins, roots, iron and lead joints, heavy greenish cables which spread and disappear into darkness hold back these hands worthy of the finest necks and of the most slender limbs and these fingers which would plait light hair with gold ribbons.

And I keep within my tensed veins all the useless blood which I could have given back to him if it had pleased him. Only my thoughts make up a worried procession for his, suggesting the fragile knot which life and its effects of stark daylight threaten to cut off at any time: there would be, I mused, this marriage without bed, without name, but without law and without stage to which the dream would give its consent where the figures of our thoughts embrace in secret.

Now, even the dream, issuing too forcefully, makes him sway; once past the servile test below the heavy slabs of air in this soulless vicinity what will remain of the voluptuous couple which we might have been?

We are played at odds against each other by fate whose bad silence forces us to speak and sigh ever louder, pity contends with horror for us, horror crushes us on the sharp fangs of desire, and here we are, with torn masts, driven by a movement which pretends to be natural, from the noble onto the ignoble, from the divine into the ridiculous from one edge to the other of the real bed. We are everything: we must know that this is nothing. Fate exchanges us against duration for the fake gold of pain, it skins us alive, it distributes us, it gives the famished mouth the noble quarter of the sex to devour, it sends us back from the highest fright to the lowest disgust: this vision transports me off the paths known to the soul, towards the paradoxical place where the lover can desire the elimination of the beloved, as sovereign good. If fate has a mouth it must be contorted with laughter.

He wears himself out: already his hands have faded, without this erosion I would have waited patiently in the engine room without breathing a word and without tears, but too much beauty in this shadow frightens me, made up I am afraid of last moments and if this work which I see being made was not a return, but supreme, I would have caught sight of death, which makes those who are cease to be, and then, no

no, to contend with matter again; what remains of it . . .

. which after the end, makes me moan, and shortly write,

Dioniris divinely distant,

The one who without body causes to germinate, who beyond everything

like the poet, not as man and as nothing
stirs each one of our gestures and without body
puts into motion
the Sex of Gold, no then
To throw myself carried away
by the ardour of those whom Love has struck in the back and
who struggle against the other, a god for a god and scream for

silence

Thus I hear myself screaming and begging, no sooner three words or nine have flown from my lips, than I wished I had never broken this silence which made a single tomb for us,

too late,

a sentence breaks out, and loses us in the terrible future in which I have forgotten one second too early that he will no longer be able to appear to me, once his image is exhausted:

'Will you later   *be able, to have,*

, to have, him

without having   *a conversation with*

without him knowing he no longer has

me of what to Him and me

I ask if by chance and later,

we would have, a voluptuous
couple

and I do not believe in chance,

known,

and I say: 'Will you later, // ...'

Throwing myself throwing him in the face this time when he cannot follow me. It is me now who is ruining him, I break the silence which made at least a single tomb for us:

... I ask him, on the off chance, and I do not believe in chance Then with difficulty he shakes his head in denial, with difficulty he draws open the heavy folds of

space in order to show me his gaunt chest, his vague
arms, his eyes dilated in the shadow, suffocating
I let that to be heard, which crushes us
which makes one enter what still is
What would be with what will have been,
then to make this gesture which removes me from his
death, he uses up his last strengths, (is he then . . . ? . . .
or not?) and I do not even know whether he will have
any left to return at least through the eyes of my memory from the invisible depths of the future
Oh then I lower my head, does he . . .? and then does
he know
That he is . . . or is it me pushing me to the edge
who makes him know what he cannot know with-
out   *being what he*
ceasing   *is*
is it me alone who knew and who later   *dead*
will know   *?*
Right here then I want to stop him: take me in the nest
of ashes
Adorned with the heliotrope plant. I will extinguish
                        Without the eyes   *better*
                                                         to die
What he touches, I do not despise   *better*
                        Without the body   *to see*

Beside him I watch him as he does undoes
He touches what has no soul or death

but gigantic bestiality: the engine moves at his com-
mand. *He* survives a little longer, not completely
undone O you,
Remain! let us remain! where what is done is done,
not far
from the sperm's undried source, delay me!

At this moment when his body casts a shadow, and
when I do not yet have the mourning dress, I have the
premonition of an incredible event: he is going to
attempt to go out into the world one last time; rupture
of the rupture;

is he . . .

dead? without anybody knowing but me?

The slabs of air lift, and in great shivers of expectation I hear the voice which first flung me to the surface of time propose:

'—But if you
want, between the two of us straight
away, higher, at the highest height a dazzling alliance
. . .
but if outside, after this mourning, without veil
outside the shadow
you found me to be less great?'

And what if I felled him with a dream?

No sooner would he appear than an atrocious pity
would bestride me and force me to run away from the
one whom I adored, through the sad power of memory

which repeats the hideousness of death, and through the heavy silence of his body strayed so far from my body, this would be a heavy, sad and gloomy dream, as a desire for revenge, where I would run away from the atrocious smell of the one still so Near my last desire, and whom I adore, me who am wary of Him! as of myself and of myself like the plague, if he returned dead, with elusive flesh, his perse face without visible eyes; there where the heart pulsed a hollow of a hyacinth-blue colour which exists only underground or among fake dreams, verging on its contrary, and yet absolute,

Then I would be, if I still wanted to love him, obliged to hate him, and, if he had to return, each time to forget him better. Any return would renew the departure, no sooner would I have caught sight of him than I would despair of seeing him, and with a dream then I would fell him . . . There would remain then, beneath Piety's piercing heels, some squirrel dust.

I remember him before this mourning, when he was unique and Himself, and all

at once I tear the shroud, I find him no less great, Or, straightaway,

he moves like a man who dreams near morning that he is waking up and who in order to wake up must break a stalk of sleep and graft it into another dream which brings him near the morning: he goes sliding from dream to dream and never ceases nearing the morning without ever looking up

Thus Dioniris slides from the arch-basement, and goes back up

And I, following him, feel the need to follow him, or to find him again and be with him at the crossroads of shadow and daylight at the fork of the real, or even at this unknown place, at the source of time, where the foetus discovers that he has made the womb and the dreamer dreams his egg. I would have met up with him at this turning. I hurry, I cut short, I sow my memory in my haste, I wind up in the city, the arrow does not leave the rope any faster

than me these entrails,

I I alone gold arrow will fell him without hurting him. His body will not have one single wound! I will know no rest or respite until I have attracted him towards me beyond the sky from below, as did the goddess from above in love with the boy who wanders beneath the earth

Love give me the burning strength with which I will meet up with him without losing him!

And you most perfumed most beautiful hardly visible, do you want once more that we, you and me in broad daylight on earth where the ivy spreads to life in death, swop sides in a fateful hunt I the arrow we Desire you the bird I the bird-catcher and do you want

the arrow the comma the pen to decide which of us
two puts the other to bed once more and whom once
again the other covers with earth?

And you, most apparent, the dark loving woman
too close to us, androphonous, do you want us three
once more to make a tremendous feast there between
life and non-life on the edge of Persephony where the
wild boars are piercing we the dream you the real you
the hunter

And in your arms and in my arms the entire earth
[entière]★

Or in our arms the earth as a third [en tiers]

If Desire must needs invent detachment which
keeps the Desired one alive I will invent it once more
and now, the one whom I hold here, I will let go of
him, what I grasp I lose and what I lose-at either
extremity of time I keep non-mortally

Himself equal to Himself impassive still virgin
without relation to time which surrounds him
enveloped with self incorruptible sleeping among fragrant herbs and spices twice born in order to twice
return to the chest or grave or parchment

I the arrow, I the bird-catcher in love with the wild
bird and with its wildness, I now aim at him at the
other extremity of age

You, shoot! fire me from the depths of ages, so that
I cleave through history! I dash far from here between

two thousand times what age was Dioniris yester eve and what age at memory's return and what age if I spring the chest open at a stroke and which then extreme story all astir with shivers and regrets, which makes one think of strange rare states of widowhood, of these forbidden mournings which I would have liked to enjoy, of these unheard-of losses which uplift the soul and throw secret archives topsy-turvy, with such violence that laws are expelled, bonds broken, times overturned, and chests give off their so-far sterile smell and lovers spill their sperm and children spread their excrements in a superb fabulous insemination.

Fired, I dash, I cleave, I get stuck shivering in the depths of ages at the foot of the wall of Reappearances and I throb, I look all around me, I stare, he is not in the crowd of the living, I scream faster and faster and lower and lower till my voice drops: I went too fast, I have run ahead of him? I can wait for him? my blood spilled too far? in time? I am early?

or now too late? I turn I look all around me

My heart struggles in overwhelming jolts like a squirrel's and the one I am envies the one I have been. I remember the Garden of Disappearances, the book of ivy, the tree with living fruit, the Most Near, Most Similar one who made me enjoy death, but he is not in the crowd of the dead

There he is! He, neither born nor dead, person or his perse phantom

Dioniris scarlet ageless always orphaned the one who wanders from chest to chest and always loses his way

He! and the earth stormy all around him is a waterless sea and nothing separates me from him but time and the wall of Reappearances if I had ninety or a thousand years or thirty I would be where he is where I am at this moment planted within reach of the Most Near very similar to himself hardly separated from Himself by the wall of Reappearances

Person or his perse phantom waits for me in the shadow through which my story is ahead of me and my desire drags me towards these lands without history these beds without deaths these ponds without waters where he wants to dictate to me the still sexless text which he will raise with a few adoptive marks.

I come from the depths of ages in front of a white monument full of pillars, balconies and light structures and covered in roses and ivy and I see them in veils of black and perse silk. She is there I can hear her laughing, it is the laughter of the new bride, she laughs, laughs, laughs faster and faster more and more sure and apparent more and more other and same as Him, I see her from the front, on my right, standing in front of the high fence full of flowers. He, whom I see from the back, teases her mouth with a small rose bough. He laughs, he rubs those big vertical carmine lips of hers. They laugh, knowingly, they do not see me. I am too much for them, not apparent enough. Suddenly they see me, without my doing it on purpose. The apparent stops laughing and blushes. He turns round. Both smile at me, knowingly, the apparent looks at the pleats of her long black skirt. She is all creased, she must surely be ninety years old, but she has those very black eyes and big red lips, and this equivocal ugliness makes her impossibly beautiful from such joyful pleasure. She is a woman from another age, austere and beautiful and ugly and lacklustre but striking

And now let my mouth know and dare.

He offers to take me back where I should be and there from a single blaze that the memory which makes the dead die again should be lost

And now he shows a gold key now a blank page now a capless pen and now his radiant face of a young man with several memories, and he talks to me with the incorruptible voice which compels the one who resists to want to give in and straightaway I give in I am hurled for the ungraspable must be mine never grasped closer and closer and ungraspable and I invent once more the detachment which keeps the desired one desirable

Just as each half missing its own half mates with it and they mutually embrace in their desire to merge into one single being and He mates with the other

and just as the bird-catcher misses the wild bird and in order to possess it releases it, in my desire to merge with the couple which He makes with the apparent I draw near in order to move away and in order to merge with them I peel off

and then there where the bed wanders and where the wandering makes the lovers' bed without limits, there where Peruvia brushes against and flees from Persephony, at the angle of times when sperm loses its way so that the Sex of Gold rises, by luck or dream, if I find another chest, let me open it! and neither sour-mother nor semifather but indifferent and thus god let me give him over to time once again.

My guide invites me to follow him with such a penetratingly gentle, peaceful voice that I do not know how to repeat it, the voice of one who would have seen, by dint of patience and wisdom, the upper side of the moon. And I wonder whether youth and old age are like the sides of the same star; and whether I could be loved by Him as strongly as the other is loved. He tells me that we are going back down by walking above the cage's roof. I remember having indeed seen, when I was coming back from the depths of ages, the cage from below, and thinking then that it had the same rounded shape, with its domed roof and its tense belly, as the bed which I had invented for Dioniris. It is the same kind of mad edifice, and the roof is made of glass. Dioniris points out to me that the cage is as good as new; if not new, restored, but empty and shunned by doves. We move away from the rose-filled balconies under the other's gaze. I feel embarrassed to have been

the cause of a separation, we walk on the somewhat
slippery roof treading carefully, then I see that we will
have to go down the other side the way squirrels do,
along a sheer massive wall. I am afraid, he reassures me,
he says it is doable, I am afraid, he goes in and calls me.
I wonder whether it would not have been wiser for me
to take off my shoes before setting out on the climb
downwards, my bare feet would have got a better grip
on the rough edges. But I dare not delay him. My heart
misses a beat when I brush past the absence of ground,
and the empty space outside becomes emptiness inside.
On the wall I see five squirrels stuck rigid as nails in
the rock face, but I dare not set foot on these living
objects, however tempted I may be. I remember that
then I was in Dioniris' arms who was carrying me
against his chest as if I were their son, more worried
about myself it seemed than about himself, he let himself slide on the back without letting go of me, setting
foot on the squirrels, and I was so astounded to feel the
vigour of his limbs that I thought of enjoying his tenderness only much later. I marvelled at his strength and
I wondered whether it was love which preserved or
whether it was the reappeared who know how to love,
I envied the new bride. Here I am back to the wall now,
with the mutilated deafness of the echo, thrown back
from myself to myself to grey wall to white wall to rock
face but by which voice first thrown, from which I
stem severed, barely by a comma and at the same time
by the concatenation of ages, separated. Perched among

the falling ivy and the fixed squirrels, with eyes wide open, blood suspended, sea with erect breakers which unceasingly beat my bones, I feel lonely, I see myself thrown, from time immemorial pushed aside, I mourn myself, nobody hears me in the east, in the west, forward, above, below, but my own white spectre, and this procession of squirrels.

If the wall to which I cling were a page, I would be the comma laid in the no woman's land between stones and expectation between Him and Himself between seduction and flight,[1] I would be the son whom the mother sentence disposes of.

Here I am perched near my guide, dreaming myself, at once bruising and bruised, but between one state and the other, which come out of each other as a thought comes out of a thought, I mourn myself I would like to love, I would like to have love for myself, and for my guide and for the apparent, and a unique passion for Him and the other. I could love them both together or differently or one for the other indifferently, I would love them to the point of taking them back

---

1 If he were a Christmas tree I would see the five white wolves of the veiled man in it, pinned on the spread branches, and I would utter such piercing screams that they would tumble down and crash to the ground without coming out of their state of hypnosis, then, my body striped with yellow and black, I would go for a humming stroll on their bodies.

and indifferently would kill them, always led up to the bed where death flows between bodies on bellies under lovers' arms without ever bursting mourning, but from veil to darkness and from swaddling clothes to cinnamon and rose bed and between us the superb and contrary murders which alone give time the appearance of life. He could be my semifather, she the earth as a third party, I the sprout, I could feed them or pierce them or bleed them or be their suckling, be seduced or slaughtered without fleeing without striking seduce while killing without killing in secret in public, in the earth or at sea, arouse their dramatic erections and give evasive retorts, refusal, rivalry desire always being born again from the nest of ashes set in the wall, would produce its effects, in turn worrying comical thrilling forbidding and simultaneously, and its effects of reality, of fake, of lived time of obscenity, which would prick out and develop the offshoots from the book of incests, this way for the penis fair, that way for Plato's heights, this way for the Dream of Dreams, on both sides of the Gully of Wild Mint which closes off the skirts of Persephony as it opens them. He, Dioniris, would erect for me the spectacular death bed at the junction of sexes and generations, where I would be killed again, killed again meanwhile and simultaneously, in the same sentence, governed by the same subject I would kill I would kill I would love the young one to whom I owe life, the Inevitable, with the grace of the One who-drives-me-below-the-watery-floor, and out of this speech from the body which I lose again the book will be born, torn to shreds by these marks and commas, but not dead, but a tomb, a semifather where the son makes his nest where there is

a magni

ficent beyond where the bed wanders ceaselessly till where the lands burn or become waters but he, tomb-like Dioniris would make this bed with his eyes closed not knowing what he is doing, unknowingly, neither death nor there

which makes me write here, on his body, and from his silence, then I, now, am I not I–who want to keep alive the semidead, semifather

the

tomb

offstage?

I will swim between two thousand ages till where Peruvia is decomposed and composes Persephony, then with a real dream I will bind the inconceivable to the conceived, I will dig in the wandering bed a real bed there where plants of mourning and plants of seduction join their roots, and produce ambiguous lands, those which know how to keep alive the dead whom love claims

where the loving woman from above lends the loving woman from below the still virgin Beloved whose fragrance travels through times and makes one write

Etymology, here is the dream here is etymology

and I, the semifather; tomb; at the root of myself
and simultaneously on my elevations outside the work
at the same time work and dream of

Dioniris of me and together lost
at the same time similar and simular,
being born for death,
born for slaughterings
each semi-author of the bed-book of incests, where the
sayable dares say the unsayable

and no death then,
and no life,
and beyond memory which can know nothing,

beyond the kingdom of eyes there where all is real
that is loved all living that is willed, where the real
wakes up dreaming,
and no need for books, nor keys, nor symbols,
but only the inexhaustible ink, the white stream, the
sperm of gold,
and no need for pages ...

Here I am; now suspended where the visible hesi-
tates and resembles the Invisible, not far from the abyss
where gemstones grow and precious bodies sleep,
where the insidious dead vegetate, who can forget that
they are dead.

And now descended not far from the gully of wild
mint where the body of the first woman lover is tram-
pled underfoot by the new bride, then this is where, in

the still virgin depths, Love distils the mixture of earth and semideath and makes rise the frankincense which troubles limits

very close to the breast where the gold embryo throbs in the place time which is linked neither to the eternal nor to History, the only point of inscription which absolutely escapes the destiny of things, a divine, unwearying point, time does not affect it, the air does not tarnish it, memory does not alter it, it is at the vanguard beyond hope of desire, to which it clears contrary and simultaneous layers and other layers where incests germinate and seedlings ripen which buried lovers cause to sprout up from the impassive body down below, where those held back by neither time nor death make love, the bird-catchers, the wild lovers, the unwearying beloveds, those without bodies who in order to desire once more and once again carve another body for themselves out of the canvasses of memory, or who wander mingled among fragrant herbs and spices or who pierce graves with their sexes of gold. No sooner have I touched the earth's lips than it sets my senses ablaze and I burn with the desire of sinking into it, I dig, it resists me and yet sucks me in,

and the dark ardent beds where Love raises the one, with two births, Adonis twice mortal issuing from death

I charge along, I pierce it, I chase while lifting trails of anemones, the smell of myrrh guides me, I cross the forests of beans with hollow stalks through which pass those among the dead who want to return, and farther I charge along and cleave down the middle the under-earths where sexes ferment and mingle

I bore into the Desire which has led me here till the end of my prenatal Peruvia a lived and reliving line, right on my unlimited body, up to the Dream of Dreams the one which proves to be real where I am a handsome man without ceasing to be a beautiful woman, and where I can die without ending life; and it is this line gradually which is what no longer needs to be a bed-book, or a tomb,

Which is a single worldsheet

and a half-buried squirrel, in the Garden of Disap-pearances, comes to my mind . . . I dig fast now, the etymological body of the absolutely earthy and mar-vellously geological earth, *Tombe* being nothing but a very weak metaphor with its writing pad its volume of parallel pages, for the infinite stratification of this planet which bears the Histories of peoples, veiled only by its actual surface but

unforeseeable, inevitable, I dig harder and harder, and poetically, the earth defending itself, all astir, trem-bling, its enormous muscles tensed, I need to slip beneath enormous packs of knotted fibres in order to find the soft earth where to dig my hole, it does not want me either, I crawl beneath the hoops of the underground trees which coarsely stitch together the mangled pieces of earth, and I am coming back to etymology, where I charge among the gold roots and ploughing the perse sides myself I spill over and cull from the chest's infinite chest and I move forward against the grain of history while waking up the lands with the stubbornness of wild mint which weeps for ninety days. The chest is there exactly at the fold of the dream when the dreamer pulls it down in order to seal it. It is impossible not to open it. Imagine the passion of wild Lovely Mint which demands the beloved at its breast and tears itself apart with its hands in order to wrench it from the chest it envies.

There he is! Still humid, the lands wrapped all around him in anemone sheets, his green limbs and crimson face being born already leaving childhood behind him, son of more than one sourmother and of Himself through Himself with Himself born, small, fragile, much loved, unique and other, already turning,

I open, there he is born from the opening to the opening already ripening the one whom no chest keeps, son of no gestation,

in one stroke of desire no sooner sown than risen and ready to race but with a face too gentle impassive and calm and destinal how old is he for Love as old as Achilles for death the same age to be born the age Dioniris was for me and to die being born and make death envy the grave; he is three years old or thirty and the entire story is behind him. He is too pale, almost too old, crowned with an immense head of hair which

tumbles in curls about his shoulders and no scissors
have touched him. He already pretends to be no more
than a child, but I can see many another time in his
eyes. He is appearing for the seventh or hundredth time,
seven or a hundred times dreamt then dismissed on
waking up. I envy the chest which I could have been
for him. His head hurts, he must have fallen, or else he
never stops falling. I manipulate him, I make him fall
heavily on his forehead, he falls off my hands. The shock
is so hard that he cries out. I pick him up gently, certain
now that he is going to die, my eyes, my sex, my lips
get moist with tenderness. I see him doomed: above
the forehead, under the curls, a double, enormous, cleft,
deadly bump: open. Did I drop him? Did he not fall
on his already wounded forehead? He smiles at me: he
begins loving me as mysteriously as if he were a semifather or my maternal uncle, from the concealed fold
of his being in my dreams, and I, deeply moved, clasp
him to my bosom, until he gets crushed, penetrates me,
merges with my passion. So Adonis feeding the heart
of his nurse. And I run away farther, with the returned
child and the son I could have had or been, and who
has effaced himself, not without changing me, now,
tomb or semifather pierced with illusions, chest of delicious monsters, snatcher of instantaneous children, lover
of those three times more mortal than me and more
alive than myself, who were born for sacrifices and the
days to come,

poet, death-work, I flee from all the children I have never had and who I could be thus I am the natural slope of time, the one which falls away: from all sides beings spring up whom the slope hurls downwards, men women carried away in spite of themselves, in an allegorical movement. Only the children run happily, still intoxicated by the laws which the elder dread. A few steps away from me, an immediate, hybrid child clad in a black yellow-striped vest runs in zigzags. It is a small swallowtail, it fascinates me, I realize that, taking advantage of the slope, my body has set out in pursuit of the small beetle. It is a handsome child, full of health, lively and desirable the delicious Dioniric demon drags my heart along the natural slope, I hold on to his running by my perverse nerves, I see him galloping, I chase him, he laughs, I raise my hand to catch him, I have never seen his face, if he was hideous or without strength? and I suspend the gesture, I content myself one more moment with the pleasure of the hunt, in his running he is perfectly handsome, he runs faster and faster, with peals of unrestrained laughter, fearlessly unaware, he runs faster and too much faster, he will fall. I know it. I could overtake him to stop him. He will fall, I will just have to lean over he will have fallen because of the slope, now he looms up and turns, I could hold him back, he staggers, and I shudder, and his curl-covered head plummets towards the natural earth, I see the full length of him collapse flat on his belly, and the shock is so hard that she trembles and startles me. He does not cry but keeps silent out of fright, pitifully. If he has hurt himself badly or killed himself how many tears I will shed on myself! When I delicately flip him over with the tip of my foot to see his face at last, one recognizes him: it's Adonis, such as he would have been, in a stageless life and outside lands, Dioniris' son, I recognize the blend of features beneath the thin veil of blood.

We are of the same stock and the same oriented river flows through us. O You, me! O me your memory you my warning, being to me like yourself, let me keep you secretly close, but neutral and sent back: I take a shovel, I dig a hole beside him; in which,—I wrap him up in paper—in next to no time I half-bury him—and with his body I bury myself and drag along with me many other dangerous and adorable little phantoms through whom I want to return later once more,

I draw the gold draperies over us, and to all of us, Dioniris, me and the other, the three of us and all the delicious monsters whom I could have been if it had been me altogether Other and in particular me or semi-me Dioniris the Unique

and the others in me who agitate me and get annoyed for not being born and all those whom I substitute for being, and those who irritate me for being who I could be if by Dioniris I was still sown in more than one bed-book, we are all carried away and just as the pollen from the wild fig tree fertilizes the cultivated fig tree and the comma of gold penetrates the textamant, and just as the drowned lover loosens the watery floor and turns it crimson, so does the desire for Love startle the *Tomb(e)* once again, splits it and overturns it and the Dream in itself comes out,

Let him who wants to have the wild dove open the cage, and if you want to have Dioniris, open the earth, cleave the text down the middle and

There he is! staggering out, all withdrawn still and with his eyelids lowered but without trace without wound without history without appearance of death without apparent

Now in one stroke He fertilizes the Tomb, the chest, the Dream in itself and the text becomes wild and follows the swing which Love gets going.

I have adored Dioniris I want him, there is no full stop or comma of the text I want Dioniris I have mourned him not one letter nor blank single sigh or silence of no struggle or peace from my body to his but absolute Love has produced,

I thought that I had felt everything extremely cried out very loud and wept even more and torn the bonds which hold the spirits in parts of the body, that I had been Love's master-pupil, and the lips and song of his voice, in reality, under several thousands of suns and as many moons . . .

Now when the Dream of Dreams took and dreamt me, in the vicinity of my story, I lived the Dream in itself, whose power is such that no land and no sea would resist its uplift, and myself carried away, with scattered limbs, history undone like hair, spilt on my gigantic traces, all the gold of the world compressed into the spark of one single gaze, I Have.

Never did I love so powerfully but for dreaming still and dreaming the Dream of Dreams, as if Love killed me in order to give me life, through a marvellous retrospective cancellation of the dantext which I had mistaken for life. I have known the orgasm of the soul which knows no rest until it dies, which makes a single untearable white sheet out of the world and no body then, except the one the earth makes for itself by convulsing the Sex of Gold.

I am here, a character ahead of its Self, and all the others whom I vaguely am, a procession of shadows bustling with the desire of being mine, and me being Dioniris'

Be the Dream and my body in echo for me.

I have never loved anybody so much, I have, Dioniris, hardly loved so much I who have come near death through him, than He himself hardly born, hardly awake, got out of the real bed with the insidious charm of those who do not know that they will be returning, stripped of human garments, too divine to fear. Therefore fear entirely mine. He, from having returned, believes himself to be definitive, outside death from now on similar to childhood for him. I, musing and facing the troubled surface of things, which the one who has loved will still love, as well as the one who is dead, however he might have returned on the watery floor, yet and yet again will founder. Something fatal in him lived only for dying and only I musing about the way the dead can believe themselves to be alive—just as the unloved lover can believe himself to be adored— I knew and yet loved him all and his death with him, but each second rejected among the living where nothing is loved more than life itself, and yet I loved him more than life.

There he is, outside death similar to his phantom, knowing something else in another time otherwise granted, move, move, down which way of myrrh and slow, troubled and immutable ivy

Larger than life, very slim, adolescent, somewhat smiling, in the role of Adonis, his bearing worthy of a king, but without authority, and with blurred flesh,

(My joy: a killing of years and desires, through the Sole Desire that everything be lived for the moment, any life poured from one body to the other before another death.) Alive more than human Himself by Himself with Himself simple and incorruptible without mouth the One who neither eats nor drinks but feeds on smells and frankincense and without sex (To embrace him! To fill myself with his presence yet without making love with him. To sleep against him, to know the appearance of death, to have him for myself all night, and to make out of one Night the product of all time.) I recognize the skin which clothes him, always the same, cut out of some dry silky crepe de chine, and fragrant; the slow progression of those not hastened by memory; he seductive and impassive moves forward and already time causes a rift in the dream of dreams, I grow old, how old is he on whom time does not weigh? Slow and absent-minded if he becomes mine what would happen to the desired one? I catch him,

I pull him by the hand,

I pull him by the hand, he resists, I insist, I tense up, he gives in, I give in hastily. I give him back. Let him be taken back and lose me, my desire takes place in the one he wants to be High, narrow, elegant, a phantom clad in silks, stubborn, somewhat smiling; but without mouth and without sex

> I hold on to him by the chest and he to me by the smell
> and each on to the other by the same gold linen
> For him I would erase all the books which he made me write,
> At last the bedchamber moves towards us with the lulling grace of a boat
> Nothing simpler: a room, a bed, but intoxicated and wild
> I do. Nothing white enough for him. The sheets become yellow and crumpled ordinary rags

However, before my eyes, lavish Dioniris expends an extravagant amount of energy: while I prepare the unique virgin, now he takes the leaves of the notebook which I have long carried on me to jot down the precious words: it is Dioniris' notebook, where the mark of love is set everywhere, but which no death had touched yet. *He* rips out a leaf and covers it with his writing. He bends me over his work: it is a direction for use by the generation whose main lines he sketches out. I see his handwriting and my throat runs dry. He rips out another leaf, his hand waved with the nimbleness of a squirrel, another sheet still bears the precious signs, I pick them up, there are ten of them and soon twelve then thirty-three, finally I do not count the handwritten copies, and I painfully remember the times when I had one single copy of his real handwriting only. It is blue. I, fascinated. The ink is blue, my sorrow marvels. A blue gold rolls. Too much wealth after too much dryness. With all this sperm he could have begot thousands of children other than me . . . but none would have carried him away so far, offstage, he writes and the ink's fragrance wafts above our heads, I bend over, and the ink flows to my mouth, its taste a little salty I suck it, its smell recognizable above all others

With what speed I finish preparing the bed-chamber! I unroll the worldsheet which covers the floor, the walls the ceiling with one single sea-land lined with Persian Self [*Soi*]★ and carbon paper, and with gold made linen [*or fait lin*].★

Nothing from here can be written any more but I drink it

Dream: I am lying against Dioniris. We still rest in the book. He puts me between his legs and I am his sex,

His bow is drawn stiff and I am his arrow
I stick ten million commas onto the world-sheet,
He lifts himself up,
And I fall back

September 1970

ancre

  1) anchor

  2) homophone of encre: ink

aimant

  1) magnet

  2) lover

  aimant(e): loving man (woman)

—> aimantant

  1) magnetizing

  2) homophone of aimant tant: loving so much

amer (fem. amère): bitter, adapted to 'sour' in l'amère

—> l'amère:

  1) homophone of la mère: the mother, hence 'the sourmother'

  2) see mer

corps-envie: see **envie**

couler

  1) to flow

  2) to sink

d'hors, d'Hors: see **ores**

effrère (from effroi: scare + frère: brither): scarebrother

entière: see tiers

envie

  1) desire, also adapted to 'lust'

  2) homophone of en vie: alive, in life

    —> corps-envie: cf. encore en vie: still alive

épère (from épée: sword + père: father): swordfather
—> l'épère: homophone of les pères: the fathers

ivoire

  1) ivory, adapted to 'icy'

  2) homophone of y voir: (I) see in it

l'hier: see **lierre**

l'ivre: see **livre**

lierre

  1) ivy

  2) homophone of l'hier: (the) yesterday, hence adapted to 'yester eve'

  3) homophone of lit erre: bed wanders

lin

   1) linen (also flax)

   2) homophone of l'un: the one

—> lin seul: as lin, seule

   1) linen, alone

   2) homophone of linceul: shroud

lit

   1) bed

   2) (s/he) reads

      —> relit, relis: (s/he) rereads, (I) reread

   3) homophone of lie: (s/he) binds

      —> relie: (s/he) binds again

—> litvre

   1) (from lit: bed + livre: book): bedbook

   2) as litvrer (from lit: bed + livrer: to give over, betray):

      to bedtray

livre

   1) book

   2) homophone of l'ivre: the drunken (one)

menthe: mint

—> la menthe

   1) homophone of l'amante: the (female) lover, hence 'the
      lovely mint'

   2) homophone of lamente: laments, hence 'pine for love'

or

   1) gold

   2) (syllogistic conjunction): now (or untranslated)

3) homophone of hors: out(side)
or fait lin:
1) gold makes/made linen
2) homonyme of orphelin: orphan
—> Orphélin: Orphée (Orpheus) + orphelin (orphan), hence 'Orphean'

—> d'or: see **ores**

ores: d'ores
1) henceforth, from now/then on
2) homophone of d'hors: of/from outside, out-
3) homophone of d'or: of gold

parchemin
1) parchment, also adapted to 'scroll'
2) homophone of par chemin: by way, also adapted to 'strolling'
—> par chemin (d'air ou terre): st/crolling (by air or land)
par quel chemin: down which way (lit.: path)

pers
1) perse
—> persant (from pers + perçant: piercing): persing
2) homophone of père: father

soi
1) self
2) homophone of soie: silk

T'extamant / textamant (from texte + amant): variation on testament (see 'Prologue', p. 7)

tiers: en tiers

   1) as a third (party)

   2) homophone of entière (masc. entier): whole, entire

     —> tout en tiers: entirely as a third party

tombe

   1) grave (also for tombeau), tomb

   2) fall, also adapted to 'tumble'

     —> tombé: fallen (to one's grave)

   3) *Tombe* (the book's title) is sometimes contextually adapted to *Tomb(e)*

voile

   1) (masc.) veil

   2) (fem.) sail